About the Author

Mark began his writing career in the business world. In 2005, he wrote *Flight of the Mayflower* which attracted excellent critical and reader reviews. In 2019 to 2023, Mark wrote two books back to back, *Born in a Storm* and *Kenny*. He has already commenced a fourth novel, *Selina Conscious*. After travelling the world and residing in three countries, Mark now lives in a leafy suburb of Brisbane, Australia.

KENNY

Mark Carew

KENNY

Vanguard Press

VANGUARD PAPERBACK

© Copyright 2023
Mark Carew

The right of Mark Carew to be identified as author of
this work has been asserted by him in accordance with the
Copyright, Designs and Patents Act 1988.

All Rights Reserved

No reproduction, copy or transmission of this publication
may be made without written permission.
No paragraph of this publication may be reproduced,
copied or transmitted save with the written permission of the
publisher, or in accordance with the provisions
of the Copyright Act 1956 (as amended).

Any person who commits any unauthorised act in relation to
this publication may be liable to criminal
prosecution and civil claims for damages.

A CIP catalogue record for this title is
available from the British Library.

ISBN 978 1 83794 131 5

This is a work of fiction. Names, characters, businesses, places, events and
incidents are either the product of the author's imagination or used in a
fictitious manner. Any resemblance to actual persons, living or dead, or actual
events is purely coincidental.

*Vanguard Press is an imprint of
Pegasus Elliot Mackenzie Publishers Ltd.*
www.pegasuspublishers.com

First Published in 2023

**Vanguard Press
Sheraton House Castle Park
Cambridge England**

Printed & Bound in Great Britain

For Kimberley

Prologue

'Why don't we simply share the lessons we have learned?' The boy asked his father. 'I mean, based on everything we have seen for the past two hundred years, the Earthlings can't evolve on their own.'

'We want to share our culture and technology,' the man replied with a kind smile, 'but it doesn't work that way.'

The man loved that his son was socially engaged at such a young age. He also knew that the Galactic Counsel developing-world interaction policies were formed over eons of hard-learned experience.

'For hundreds of thousands of years,' the man continued, 'we have seen countless civilisations reach a point of development then stop evolving. When we try to help, it ends in disaster.'

'That doesn't make sense,' the boy said. 'Why can't they be helped?'

'It's because on planets like Earth, good, fair-minded, and honest people don't want to run giant corporations or become political leaders,' his father told him. 'Only egotists, sociopaths and criminals do.'

The boy was stunned. This knowledge made him very sad.

'Galactic history has proved infinitum that some life-forms in the galaxy don't care who leads them, as long as they have lots of food, fancy cars and big screen TVs.' The man finished his thought.

'So, we just sit in space and watch the Earthling politicians protect a handful of greedy billionaires destroy their own planet?' the boy asked.

'Obviously this topic is close to your heart, so I'm going to tell you a story,' the man began.

The boy loved stories. He sat up in his chair and focused on his father's words.

'During a rainstorm, a scorpion was washed away and ended up on the wrong side of the river. He wondered if he would ever see his family again, who were all on the other side of the river, and the scorpion couldn't swim.'

'Why couldn't he swim, Father?' The boy asked.

'I don't know. Maybe he didn't take swimming lessons,' the man replied patiently.

'He should have learned and he wouldn't be in this situation,' the boy quipped.

'If you are going to interrupt me on every point, this will be a very long story,' the man patiently told his son.

'Sorry, Father.'

'While the scorpion sat on the bank worrying about his family, a deep despair overcame him. Then, at his very lowest moment, a frog arrived.'

'A frog?' Kenny asked. 'Do you mean like a green river frog?'

'Yes, Kenny, a fucking green river frog.' His father drew a deep breath.

Twenty years later...

Kenny thought about the story of the scorpion and frog many times over the years. Although he understood the concept, it completely failed to resonate with his core beliefs.

The scorpion begged the frog for a ride across the river, only to sting the frog half way across, and they both drowned. As his father explained; scorpions sting. It's what they do.

'You can't change the nature of things,' Kenny whispered to himself. 'Well, that's just a pile of gutless obfuscation bullshit. I can change the Earth and I'll write a PowerPoint presentation to prove it!'

***

Galactic Star Ship (GSS) Mercurial Blue
Classification: Military, Non-Combatant
Mission: Observe and broadcast Earthling activities to the galaxy
Crew: Seabertian nationals. 20 fleet officers and 100 enlisted crew
Position: Planet Earth, Reba Station

Tour Rotation: Three years
The Surface Mission
Tuesday Morning

As Lieutenant Alicia breezed into the Data Interception Centre (DIC), she caught her reflection on the glass wall and smiled.

Alicia had an innate ability to catch her own reflection in almost any reflective surface. Her friends said it was her true super-power.

In one graceful movement, she performed a little pirouette and landed on her brand new 'ergo-smart' flight chair.

The manufacturer of the chair named it 'Joot' in an ambitious effort to make it seem more friendly.

Sensing Alicia's body profile, Joot whirred in contentment as he moved foam and latex to match her contours.

Joot failed. Alicia's butt was simply too perfect for his limited programming.

'These smart chairs are dumber than my grandmother's ort,' Alicia complained. The Seabertian word 'ort' is a noun for the small piece of skin found between Seabertian sex organs and the anus.

After much squirming and complaining, Alicia finally found a setting she could live with, and began watching CNN's live broadcast of Jethro Cox's historic sub-orbital space hop. Alicia viewed the video feed of Jethro Cox and his posse of self-proclaimed billionaire astronauts board their rocket with disdain. The ship reminded her of a fat man's penis, a hopelessly white and uncared for puggy phallus.

'Appropriate,' she muttered.

'What is?' Lieutenant James asked her from the next console station.

'I'm looking at a giant white penis filled with old men who haven't seen their dicks since 1996,' she told James.

'Oh, good for you,' he told her.

James had grown accustomed to Alicia by this point. He rarely knew what she was talking about, yet was oddly satisfied with that.

Alicia switched her screen to the social media feed, and read live posts as they appeared.

Essentially, every post was one of hope and desire: hope that the penis-ship would explode in the Earth's atmosphere, and a desire that Jethro Cox would die screaming.

This vision made Alicia smile. She knew the Earthlings hated Jethro Cox, as several posts affirmed this fact.

"Cox is a renowned tax avoider and slave labour-force owner. He buys outrageous toys for his own personal gratification while his workers relieve themselves into bottles on the factory floor."

She watched the countdown, also hoping the white penis would explode.

'I honestly have no idea what we're doing here,' James intoned, stretching his back and yawning.

'We're observing, numb nuts,' Alicia intoned. 'Didn't you read your job description?'

'But how did we get Earth?' James complained. 'Everyone else from the academy was assigned fun planets like Splashmegathor, the waterpark planet. Or Floatasia, where you float around all day drinking cocktails and smoke hand-rolled litagithum leaves waiting for gen-rapture.'

While James indulged in his favourite activity of wishing and dreaming, Alicia focused on the launch. The countdown terminated and the white penis left the pad. It climbed in a perfect arc toward its assigned point in space.

'That's crap!' Alicia swore and swiftly lost interest. 'To your original question, little Jimmy, about why we are here. The answer is simple. You are a serial fuck-up, and I wouldn't sleep with critical members of the flight assignment committee,' she said, adjusting her flight suit again. 'I swear, whoever designed these uniforms needs to be flogged with a busan-lumbinious tail.'

'The assignment guys didn't miss anything. I hear you're lousy in the sack,' James told her.

'True,' Alicia replied. 'Though when you look like me, you can screw like a wet mattress and get away with it.'

James turned his head and looked at her. For two solid years Alicia had given him hot sweats and night tremors; now she was just part of the furniture.

'Where's that dickhead Kenny?' James asked, not actually caring.

Alicia shrugged and offered an unhelpful grunt. She was busy compiling the Earthling newsfeeds that were due upstairs an hour ago.

From their rotational orbit, fifty thousand miles above the Earth, the huge Seabertian star ship viewing window gave Alicia a tremendous vista.

'Such a pretty planet,' she mused. 'Green and blue, lots of water, and potentially clean air. All wasted on the Earthlings.'

'What's that?' James asked.

'Nothing,' Alicia said. 'I'm just thinking about what to have for lunch.'

'Lunch?' James asked. 'You just ate breakfast!'

'Fuck you, James,' she swore. 'A girl needs to keep up her strength.'

In the ship's main dining mess, Commander Kenneth Kendrick had three ensign-rank junior officers baled up while he practiced his pitch on them.

The ensigns did their best to look interested, while individually considering the many ways they could kill themselves. Kenny continued droning, in excruciating detail, about how he could save the Earthlings from themselves.

The junior officers knew, along with every other sentient entity in the galaxy, from reptiloids to stylopids, that planet Earth was a write-off. So, what in the name of Glandor's massive twort was Commander Kendrick flapping his gums about?

The Earthlings had missed all of their critical crossroad opportunities to evolve. Being complete arseholes, they invariably chose the path of expedience and corruption. Now their demise was all but inevitable as they became dumber by the day, and their leaders more and more corrupt.

As the galactic song went: "Puff, puff, puff, go the coal fires. Ching, ching, ching flows the money."

When he finished speaking, Kenny sat back and waited.

Nothing.

'Come on, people! What do you think?' he encouraged them.

'Grand plan, sir,' Ensign Kyle told him.

'I can see how that might work, sir,' Ensign Rebekah added.

'Er, great plan, sir. But I'm not sure the colonel will let you do it,' Ensign Amanda told him.

'Finally!' Kenny shouted. 'Someone was brave enough to say it. Well done, Ensign Amanda!'

He jumped to his feet and marched out of the dining mess.

The trio let out a sigh of relief. They all thought Commander Kenny was a complete lunatic, but he signed their performance sheets and if they ever wanted a proper assignment, they had to suck it up.

Kenny made his way to the Data Interception Centre and sat at his console.

'Where have you been?' James asked. 'No, wait. Let me guess. Practising your stupid pitch on helpless squabs.'

'James,' Kenny began. 'You must realise that due to the strict limitations of your breeding, having been spawned from contaminated sperm from a South-East Central Tractearain waste transfer station bargain-price male whore, and a mother who owns forty cats, that you have neither the intellect nor the creative capacity for intergalactic problem solving.'

James smiled. He liked that one.

'True,' James replied. 'But then I wasn't passed around the breast-feeding circle of inbred, genetically modified cum-buckets from the homogenised nest of wasps that hive-swarmed in the West Celestina Golf Club owned by your fully corrupt, uncle-fornicating father. A sad and twisted little man, who was recently arrested in a public toilet tag-team jerk circle with three-dicked Tritanopes.'

'That was, and still is, just a rumour,' Kenny declared. 'Besides, everyone knows daddy prefers two-dicked Catalonians.'

'You two idiots need a new act,' Alicia complained. 'Your shit was funny for the first two years, now it's just sad.'

'So, what's happening down there?' Kenny asked.

'Oh, you know, the usual nonsense,' Alicia told him. 'Rich shitbags are blowing billions of dollars, and themselves, into space while kids starve. Their world gets hotter while they commission more coal-fired power stations. The Americans are baiting the Chinese and the Russians, desperately seeking a new war after they completely fucked the Middle East. The forests are burning in Southern California, Australia, South America, and South-East Asia. Oh, and you'll love this: CERN and the Chinese are building mega particle-colliders. When asked, "How will you contain the anti-matter?" they both said, "Don't worry about that, it's all under control."

Kenny scratched his head. He knew it was time to act. His plan was sound, and he'd perfected his pitch. It was time to nut-up or shut up.

'Don't wait up, children. Daddy will be late,' he told his team.

They both turned around and watched Kenny leave.

'Does that fucker do any work around here?' Alicia asked the closing door.

As Kenny walked, he marvelled at the *Mercurial Blue*. It was a modern ship, fitted-out for long haul, deep space tours of duty. The gangways and communal spaces were lit in blue-tinged hues, a colour deemed most relaxing, and soothing to the soul.

The dining mess, crew lounges, gyms and spas, housed wall-sized screens that ran loops of placid oceans, excessively green forests, or mixed-gender swimwear competitions, depending upon on the emotional state of the artificial intelligence environment control computer.

One week previously, the AI computer woke up in foul mood and ran loops of Earthling car crashes for an hour before the tech team could provide counselling for the depressed machine.

On this day, or at least, at this moment, Kenny was enjoying a rare feeling of personal empowerment. He had a plan. He knew he was right, and he was ready to take a huge gamble.

As he rode the elevator to deck five, Kenny sang a tune that had implanted itself deep inside his head. The song by Dire Straits explored the wonders of getting your money for nothing and your chicks for free.

'That's a laugh!' Kenny scoffed. In his experience, making money was a bitch and chicks cost a fortune.

Kenny liked to sing, and knew in his heart he could have been a great rock star. This belief was shared mostly by his mother, and a spotty girl named Linda in eighth-grade maths with a hyperactive gland disorder. Linda loved Kenny and wanted to be his girlfriend.

What his mother, and Linda, failed to acknowledge was Kenny's moth-like attention span. He had an inability to engage with anything he did not personally invent. He also deeply despised repetition.

This combination of personality traits, of course, was the absolute antithesis of the requirements for learning a musical instrument.

The elevator ride terminated at the office of the ship's commander, where Kenny strode forth with a glint in his eye.

He was on fire and he knew it.

'I need to see Colonel Hipu at his soonest convenience,' Kenny told the colonel's personal assistant, Karen.

Karen viewed Kenny as a Galenian mega-toad may view a Leonida holiday beetle. Nobody hated these toads for their dietary love of the Leonida beetle. For, although being cruel and unfeeling toward these sweet innocent beetles, the Galenian toads went on to invent a better, longer lasting swimming pool filter.

'And what may I tell the colonel is the nature of your request?' a tight-lipped Karen intoned.

'An actionable interplanetary strategic intervention proposal,' Kenny said, then placed his face on screen-saver mode. He hated Karen with all his heart, and wanted to kick her in the DeJong, but refused to give her the pleasure of knowing that.

"DeJong" is a horrendously derogative Seabertian noun derived from the galactically ubiquitous male desire for flavoured peach. It's mostly spoken by males when feeling cranky against females, and who are brave enough to utter such a bold and inflammatory exclamation.

Needless to say, speaking the word DeJong out loud often ends in a good slapping.

'Can you give me any more information?' she asked in her very best cold lizard voice.

'No.'

He waited while Karen stared at him. He then waited some more until Karen realised Kenny had shut the conversation down. Karen held his gaze for a few more seconds before making an elaborate performance of checking the colonel's calendar.

During this excruciating process, Kenny stood before her completely impassive. He knew if he complained, spoke, or even moved, Karen would have the upper hand. This was hard for Kenny, as he was not famous for maintaining self-discipline.

What really got Kenny's goat was the knowledge that the colonel was always available. In his role of commanding an orbiting observation ship, the colonel had absolutely nothing to do.

In a moment of extreme boredom, Kenny had hacked the colonel's web browser history and discovered he watched a disproportionate amount of Earth-porn. Quite a lot of this porn was very disturbing and not legal in most of the known Galaxy.

Kenny, though, could not help but be impressed with the Earthlings' range of sexual perversions. In his mind, a species that displayed this level of creative sexual depravity was definitely worth saving. It never occurred to him that the Earth-men were simply bored and that their wives hated them.

'The best I can do is let the colonel know you want a meeting,' Karen informed him stiffly.

'Most kind,' Kenny replied with a harsh grimace. He turned on his heels and marched away.

'Horrendous crow,' he muttered while still in earshot.

'Pretentious twat,' she told his departing back.

Twenty-four hours passed and there was still no word from the colonel. So much porn and so little time, Kenny guessed. He knew it was time to be bold.

The colonel did his rounds of the ship every morning at ten sharp. Kenny chose a favourable position and lay in wait. He positioned himself in the gangway between the operations and engineering spaces where he knew the colonel would be approaching.

Bingo! Right on time the colonel entered Kenny's stakeout, and the look on the man's face was not pleasant.

'Commander Kendrick! Why is my DIC supervisor coming out of the engineering spaces?'

'Our head was occupied, sir. I prefer to take my morning dump in engineering anyway. Leave it where it belongs, I've always said.'

'Is that a joke?' The colonel's face began to flush with hues of pink and red. He was a big beefy man who had spent most of his career in the frontlines of new planet exploration as the brigade commander in the infamous Red Devils assault rangers.

Only the hardest of men and women served with the Devils, as they were the first ones dropped onto newly discovered worlds, and were rarely welcomed with opened arms. In fact, the majority of "arms" that welcomed them held spears, clubs and blow-darts.

On the day of the colonel's last battle, he was overseeing the mop-up of a long and deadly battle against the Leticerian hordes of tree-dwelling, cave-inhabiting and plains-riding creatures.

In fact, the fuckers were everywhere.

The Leticerians were famous for eating everything that wasn't Leticerian. Except, of course, when they ran out of food. Then they also ate fellow Leticerians. But only the juicy ones.

This became their downfall, as in battle, when they managed to kill a Red Devil, they would take a break and start eating themselves a little Devil meat.

Fresh is best, was the famous old Leticerian saying.

One night, after a long day of slaughter, the colonel left the security of his camp to take a piss. It was then that a rogue Leticerian jumped down from a tree and hurled a spear at him.

The colonel was in his prime and caught the spear, throwing it back at the attacking Leticerian. Much to the colonel's surprise, the Leticerian caught it and hurled it back at the colonel, thus starting the first game of chuck and catch in that part of the galaxy.

The game was short lived after the Leticerian became bored and gave the colonel a full facial spray of Leticerian squirt urine. From this one cowardly stream of piss, the colonel never fully recovered.

It is said, a Leticerian will only squirt under one of two circumstances: to totally fuck-up an enemy in hand-to-hand combat, or to win a party bet. Distance, volume and accuracy win the big points, or so the story goes.

Leticerian urine contains a concentrated, heavy element hallucinogenic that induces post-traumatic flashbacks in its victim forever. Long after death, rotting corpses have been seen jumping to their feet and barking like dogs.

People had actually heard the colonel barking under conditions of extreme stress, or after eating Mengerian fired beans. The gas the colonel's body produced in the digestion of the beans was quite toxic when combined with Leticerian squirt urine.

In any other situation, this debilitating condition would have seen the colonel pensioned off. Yet, lucky for him, he had friends on the flight assignments board who allowed him to finish his career somewhere harmless and completely pointless. So, they sent him to Earth.

Kenny knew this and needed to be careful. If the colonel became upset, he could pluck out one of his eyes. The colonel had done this more than once, as many a one-eyed junior commander could testify.

'No joke, sir. I had the runs from eating too many zliger berries. I don't think the galley reconstituted them at the correct temperature and the fermentation—'

'Enough!' The Colonel barked. 'I know why you want a meeting. Everyone on board this piss-weasel of a ship knows! But let me tell you right here and now, sonny boy, your plan is stupid and I don't want to hear it!'

'Begging the colonel's pardon,' Kenny persisted. 'How can you possibly know exactly how stupid my plan is if you've never heard it? Please give me five minutes and I will demonstrate beyond doubt the level of its stupidity.'

The logic of Kenny's argument shocked the colonel, causing him to suffer a Leticerian squirt twitch.

If I give this idiot five minutes now, I'll never have to listen to his bullshit again, the colonel reasoned.

'Go! You have five minutes.' The colonel set his watch timer.

'What here?' Kenny was appalled. 'But I have a slide show!'

'No, you fucking don't. Speak!'

Kenny pulled himself together and began his pitch.

***

The Data Interception Centre

'Ye Gods! Here we go again,' Alicia told James.

'What?' James asked, already bored to death with Alicia and her bullshit for one day.

'We're doing another flasher run.'

'Where this time?'

'It's a big one! We're doing Dallas then Fort Worth, Texas,' Alicia told him.

'Ha! I still remember the Phoenix lights in ninety-seven. What a shitstorm that caused.'

'We're flying the big disk above the city at twenty knots for an hour.' Alicia read the brief.

'What? The nine hundred footer?' James asked. 'Funny how the tech boys keep changing the shapes. Disks to oblongs, then triangles, now back to disks.'

'What shape do you prefer, wise guy?' Alicia enquired.

'You know me; I'm an arse man. What about a nice set of hovering butt cheeks?'

'It's times like these I'm glad I never slept with you,' Alicia told him. 'You're a pervert and a loser.'

'You wouldn't have sat on my face anyway, being the useless fuck-mattress that you are. So, no loss then.'

'It's started! Now watch the nine-one-one calls come in. I give the media fifteen minutes,' Alicia said keenly.

James watched Alicia work. She loved poking the humans.

'You know it's like teasing ants, don't you?' James sighed. 'You're a very sad and sorry girl, Alicia.'

She nodded and grinned, like all good sociopaths.

***

The colonel listened to Kenny's pitch and nearly plucked out his eye. The only thing that gave him pause was another tedious court marshal and corresponding prison sentence.

On the way back to his office, the colonel reached Karen's desk where he motioned her to follow him.

'Lock the door,' he told her.

'We'll have to be quick. You have a video conference with the admiral in thirty minutes.'

The colonel loosened his belt and dropped his pants. Karen plonked herself on a chair in front of him and went to work.

The young, genetically modified crew members thought Karen was a hag. The colonel, though, enjoyed her real woman looks. He hated all that superficial beauty-perfection nonsense the trigennials demanded.

In fact, he thought all trigennials looked the same. Nothing but cardboard cut-outs from the same gene enhancement company marketing department.

The colonel moaned for Karen.

Encouragement was the key to receiving a good blowjob, he knew. He placed his hand on her head and subtly moved it in time with her motion. *Never force it*, he told himself. *Karen must believe she's driving the bus.*

'Oh, my Gods!' He moaned for her again.

Five minutes later, Karen was cleaning herself up.

'You seemed a little tense today, did that little turd Kendrick find you?' Karen asked.

'He ambushed me,' the colonel told her.

'Did you listen to his bullshit plan?' Karen asked.

She enjoyed being the colonel's confidante. She knew he couldn't speak frankly with the other toss-wallys on the ship.

'Why do you think I'm so tense?' The colonel stroked Karen's hair. 'Kendrick kept going on about this stupid "catch 22" as he calls it.'

Karen shook her head. She wished she could blow Kenny out into space through an airlock.

'Kendrick keeps going on about how the Earthlings are too stupid and dangerous to join the galactic community. But if we don't help them by placing a finger on the scale, they'll just keep making the same mistakes until they kill their planet. Then nobody wins.'

'What are you going to do?' she asked him.

'Galactic interplanetary policy is very clear about interfering with developing worlds. I know we have violated that policy a few times, but whenever we try to help, it blows up in our faces.' The colonel shook his head. 'If you'll pardon the pun.'

Karen giggled for him. 'We've seen this before. You know that some worlds can't be helped,' she reminded him, and stroked his thick, strong hair. 'Maybe you should stop worrying about it. We don't want you getting over-stressed now, do we?'

The colonel smiled at Karen. She really was quite a woman.

Karen returned his smile. She knew that without her, there would be piles of plucked eyeballs up and down the gangways.

'Anyway, Kendrick's plan is pure nonsense,' the colonel told her. 'He requested to be sent to the surface as a political insurgent. The idiot thinks he can implode America's greatest internal threat and give them a chance for a new start.'

'You mean imploding their Republican Party and propaganda machine Fox News?' Karen asked.

'The trouble is, the little bastard is right,' the colonel told her.

Karen smiled as a fun thought occurred to her. 'Our race does look a lot like the Earthlings,' she began, deliberately planting a seed. 'Sure, we are taller than the average Earthling, but not freakishly so. The young officers are all genetically modified and very pretty, even the women. Our only difference is that we are dramatically over-sexed, but then so are Earthling politicians. Always sending pictures of their dicks to each other, the crude motherfuckers.'

The colonel grunted in agreement. He noticed Karen had missed a little colonel-cum on her right ear and gave it a quick wipe.

'You know,' Karen continued, 'if Kendrick did go on a surface mission, he wouldn't be on the ship.'

The Leticerian squirt urine that surged through the colonel's brain had left him a little slow-witted. Yet, he could still identify a good piece of logic when he heard it.

'I think you're onto something.' He smiled. 'I'll raise it with the admiral.'

'Yes, sir.' Karen winked at him. 'Your conference call starts in five minutes.'

'Karen, I think it's time to stop calling me sir. Also, order me some Mongenian fired beans, would you?'

'Never. They make you fart and the stench flows all the way to my office,' she replied. 'You can have a bowl of steamed Shencian liver.'

'Not Shencian liver again! Just make sure it's smothered with Haversian sauce. You know the Shencians are chronic alcoholics. Should we really be eating their livers?'

Karen smiled and shrugged. She loved the colonel. It was like owning a large, dim-witted Kantisher K9, but with slightly fewer fleas.

With a huge bowl of steaming liver in front of him, Colonel Hipu flicked on his big TV.

'Admiral Gustov! How wonderful to see you again! Have you lost weight?'

'Hipu! You are one urine-soaked masturbater! Please don't start all our calls by licking my balls.'

'Sorry, sir. I'll try to reign in the ball licking next time,' Hipu said with a smile and a wink.

'And don't wink at me! It's just fucking weird,' the admiral complained. 'I have no idea why we bother with these calls. My bosses ordered me to speak to you idiots every week, so there we have it. Do you have anything of any value for me or shall we just sit here playing with our dicks for five minutes?'

'You go right ahead, Admiral. Karen just blew me, so I'm good,' Colonel Hipu told him. 'We did another flasher run with the nine hundred foot disk today. We're still preparing them for the possibility of first contact, but there's no sign they're getting their shit together.'

'So, situation normal, all fucked up?' the admiral asked.

'Correct, sir,' Colonel Hipu said and paused for a moment. 'However, there is a new surface mission under consideration. It's likely a complete waste of time, but—'

'What mission?'

'One of my more moronic commanders has proposed to infiltrate their political leadership. He wants to embed himself with—'

The admiral released his dick and held up his hand.

'No! No! No! We are not doing that shit again!' he declared. 'You know what happened last time with the Kennedys. They shot him, and his brother. Then his youngest brother drove his car off a bridge and killed a girl, just to avoid the bullet.'

Colonel Hipu thought about this for a second. Shoot him? Shoot Commander Kendrick? The colonel smiled.

'You're right, sir,' Colonel Hipu began. 'Then again, think about the publicity and the ratings if this actually went somewhere, all for the price of one little upstart commander. I mean, everyone on the ship hates him.'

Admiral Gustov grabbed his dick again.

The ratings! He was going to retire in six months and the galactic broadcasting corporations hired ex-military leaders as lobbyists for developing-planet comedy broadcasting rights.

This could be his way in! *A real coup*, he told himself.

'The Reality Earth TV channel has always rated very well, especially in the bogan systems.' Admiral Gustov was thinking out loud and Hipu didn't interrupt him. 'The network people would love the whole first-person thing.

We could implant cameras in his eyes and sound in his ears.'

The colonel shook his head a few times. 'I'm not sure, sir. It would be asking too much of young Kendrick to risk his life after what happened last time.'

'How ambitious is this Commander Kendrick of yours?'

'Oh, very.'

'Get him in here.' The admiral leaned back on his massively oversized chair and returned to playing with his dick.

'Karen!' The colonel yelled at his intercom. 'Get Kendrick for me, right now!'

Faster than an ion-charged fart particle leaving a gaseous Horandious, Commander Kenny Kendrick was knocking on the colonel's door.

'Come in my boy! Take a seat,' the colonel purred, affording the young man a huge smile.

Kenny's sphincter puckered.

That welcome! The friendly tone of voice! Kenny knew he was in serious trouble. And oh shit! There was the admiral on the big screen with his dick in-hand.

'Commander Kendrick, I presume? I hear you're a true leader of men,' the admiral crooned.

Was the admiral actually smiling? Kenny asked himself. He didn't know the admiral could smile after being slapped in the face by a Dolphoidian waitress at the 2007 Star Core conference on the water world of Dorpe.

'Actually, sir, I only lead one man. That's if you can actually call James a man, and a skank named Alicia. I technically command three trigennial ensigns, but they're about as useful as three saucers of piss-water,' Kenny announced, his sphincter relaxing a little.

'Excellent! Excellent!' The admiral chortled. 'Space Corp needs more brave and ambitious young men like you! My Gods, in five years you'll be captain material. Now, tell be about this exciting mission you have planned.'

'I have a slide show.' Kenny beamed.

'Wonderful! Wonderful!'

***

Back in the DIC, James and Alicia were eating cake.

'Did you know,' James began, 'in the old days, pre-designer genetics that is, people actually got fat from eating cake.'

'Fuck off!' Alicia spat, blasting small bits of saliva-moistened cake from her mouth.

'No, it's true,' James replied, wiping Alicia's spit-cake off his face. 'The sugar triggered a release of excess insulin that made the body store energy as fat without burning it. That's why fat people were always hungry and kept eating more cake.'

'You really are full of it,' Alicia said as she washed down another massive mouthful of cake with a gulp of milkshake. 'Everyone knows that body fat comes from being stupid.'

James took a moment to view Alicia.

'Then how do you explain your rocking hot body?' James asked.

She threw a fork at his face.

The DIC door opened with its familiar whirr, and Kenny marched in.

'You missed out on cake, dickwad,' Alicia told him.

'It's Commander Dickwad, you skinny slag. Now shut up and listen; we have a new mission.' The pair sensed this was serious, as Kenny had never pulled rank before.

Galacticom Broadcasting Network
Head Office
Planet Zireatian in the Domellar System

On the 400th floor of the second tallest ulopian-reinforced tower in the galaxy, Geon Plume was feeling stupid and uncomfortable.

The height of the building was so extreme the engineers designed it to flex with the wind, as the stress imposed on a rigid structure would trigger its demise.

This constant swaying was not lost on the inhabitants working within. Many described it as similar to working on a cruise ship during storm season. While traditional office workers may develop repetitive strain injury or posture related back issues, Galaticom workers suffered sea sickness and scurvy.

While Geon waited in the plush outer office of the legendary Todd Splick, head of Galactic Reality TV Programming, he battled waves of building-sway nausea.

He promptly lost interest in that conundrum and sat in an over-designed leather chair that was built to both hug and squeeze its victims.

Geon judged the chair would be more at home in the lounge of a Cratornia people smuggler with a drug import side-line, and not a broadcasting executive lobby.

Geon Plume suddenly realised the chair had trapped him. The more he squirmed, the tighter the chair gripped him. In near panic, Geon said fuck it twice, and with a huge effort, using all his upper body strength, heaved himself to his feet..

He turned and stared at the chair with all the hatred he could muster.

'Try using your legs and engage your core next time,' Splick's receptionist suggested.

'A chair that requires a strength coach just to stand up. Very clever,' Geon told her.

'Yeah, it's a pretty stupid chair. In summer, it smells like the Asslonigan camel it was made from,' she informed him.

'You mean I've just been sitting on a dead Asslonigan?' Geon cried. He was beginning to hate everything.

'There's a bench over there.' The receptionist pointed to a marble slab on legs.

'That's fine. I think I'd rather stand.'

Five minutes later, Geon Plume jumped to his feet when the infamous Todd Splick came out and greeted him personally.

'Firstly, let me say what an honour it is to meet you,' Geon gushed.

'I can imagine it would be,' Todd Splick intoned, practising the new fashion accent he learned while watching the Entertainment Channel. It was a combination of gloort and vert, with a dash of klamentia.

To Earthling ears, he sounded a lot like a Welsh bog farmer's son who, from the age of twelve, was raised under the sodomy and violence regime of an expensive English boarding school. Then wasted two summers making an arse out of himself while attempting to get laid in Paris.

Geon Plume also knew Todd Splick was a galactic-level twat. Being a galactic twat-whisperer, Geon knew exactly how to handle him.

Geon performed a quick mental twat-management checklist:

Rule One: A twat is only ever interested in himself.

Rule Two: Never talk about yourself to a twat. The twat is incapable of hearing anyone speak, except themselves and other extreme twats. If in doubt, go back to Rule One.

Rule Three: The twat is always right. No matter how stupid the twat is, and they are mostly pretty stupid. Never, ever, contradict a twat. This rule extends to building upon the twat's own thoughts, or in any way adding a variance in your precis of the twat's original statement. You must always agree with the twat, word for word.

'Would you like a feign-dried olikan coffee?' Todd Splick asked Geon.

The drink was the latest trend in galactic indulgence. Olika berries are genetically modified to grow on the backs of the londer beasts that were brought back from extinction specifically for the purpose of olika berry production.

The ripening berries are plucked off the backs of the beast by extremely brave and drastically under-paid Xcremtian tribesmen. The tribesman had lost all their wealth and dignity since making a drunken and foolhardy bet with the Retreatians in the Age of Yip the Groomer.

Yip the Groomer was given that title as the man was mad about his hair.

The Xcremtian leader, a man called Flupp, bet Yip the Groomer he could unfreeze his moistened testicles from a local glacier during a celebration of the great hippoid run.

What the Xcremtian leader failed to calculate was the effect of a recent la nina weather event that delayed the coming of spring for a whole month.

Politically speaking, Plume despised the olika berry trade. But the coffee was unbelievably good and it afforded its drinker more than a slight pants-chubby.

'You're probably wondering what all the fuss is about?' Todd Splick finally got down to business.

'I must say, I've heard the rumours,' Geon said coyly.

'Cast those rumours aside, Geon, my man! I'm about to offer your ad agency the brand leadership opportunity of a lifetime. We are taking our high-rating show, *Reality Earth*, and upping the ante.'

Todd Splick scratched his balls, sniffed his finger, then grinned like a maniac.

During the ball-scratching, Geon noticed a sizable chub forming in Splick's pants from the olika coffee.

Splick was very proud of his chub, and it afforded him no end of entertainment. He constantly played with it, but only when he wasn't trying to shove it into all the humanoid and non-humanoid holes he could find. He even took photos of it to share with his social media fans.

While trying to ignore Splick's chub, Geon remembered that all TV twats put on a big show when trying to sell revamped TV shows. Yet, being a professional ad-man, Geon played along.

'So, what's the plot?' Geon asked.

'The plot? The plot is fucking amazing! That's what the plot is!' Todd Splick was now on a full olikian high. He was twitching, scratching his balls and jumping about way too much for Geon's comfort levels.

Geon sat on a chair, hoping it would calm Splick down. Sadly, it had the opposite effect. Geon found himself at dick-level with Splick, who danced around in his face space.

'Okay! You win! How much money do you want?' Geon asked, praying the meeting would soon be over.

'Geon! My man! You can suck my dick for free!' Todd Splick stopped dancing just long enough to unzip his pants.

'Oh, great Lord Mistrealian!' Geon cried. 'Kill me now!'

Mercurial Blue — Briefing Operations and Orientation Booth (BOOB)

Every flight officer serving on the *Blue* knew that Commander Kenny Kendrick was quite keen on slideshows. In fact, Commander Kenny was often heard to say that if a message can't be converted to a slideshow presentation, it wasn't a real message. Or something to that effect, as no one was actually listening.

'Hush now, people. We have work to do.' Kenny failed to gain their attention.

His young ensigns were busy watching Gala-Tube short videos of dancing cats on their devices.

Gala-Tube executives discovered that normal length videos of two to three minutes far exceeded the attention span of micro-focus trigennials. Twenty, or maybe thirty seconds was all you were going to get from these genetically modified little twats.

Alicia too was getting bored. She had a spa day booked and was starting to twitch.

'Shut the fuck up! Or I will have you little scumbags cleaning my bathroom for a week,' Alicia yelled.

The trigennials instantly fell silent. Everyone knew how much Alicia ate in a day, and the horror of cleaning her toilet struck desperate fear into their hearts.

She nodded for Kenny to proceed.

Kenny got an instant pants-chub for Alicia. Alicia saw his pants-chub and shook her head. Kenny replied with an exaggerated frowny face, but Alicia was already ignoring him.

What a DeJong Alicia is, Kenny thought.

'Righty-ho, team,' he began. 'This one comes straight from the top.'

'Who? The galactic president?' Ensign Amanda asked.

'No,' Kenny sighed.

'The chief of staff of the Admiralty?' Ensign Rebekah asked.

'No,' Kenny moaned.

Ensign Kyle's hand shot up, but he caught a full-weight glare from Alicia and quickly dropped his arm.

Kenny got another chub for her.

'This assignment comes from Admiral Gustov,' Kenny told them. 'We're going to save the Earth, and it'll be televised across the galaxy. We're talking network TV here, guys.'

'The whole galaxy, sir?' Ensign Amanda asked. 'Or just the bogan dung-traders from the Scutum-Centaurus arm? After all, we only rate well out there.'

'I'm told this broadcast will attract a much wider audience,' Kenny replied, feeling a little depressed. He hated presenting to trigennials, they all had the attention span of goldfish. But not the smart ones who learned algebra and calculus.

'That depends on how you market the show, sir.' Ensign Kylie finally got his shot in.

'Okay, I get you're a bunch of bored smartasses.' Kenny was losing his shit, and this made the ensigns happy. 'But no more questions until I'm done. Don't forget, I still have your performance reviews on my desk.'

The young officers moaned and shifted in their seats. Their fun was over, and they knew it. They now had to sit quietly and listen to Kenny's stupid presentation.

'Okay, then.' Kenny took a breath. 'As you all know, it has been my lifelong dream to help the Earthlings. As it stands, the anti-social and eco-destructive Earthling billionaires dominate their political structures aided by their right-wing media propaganda machines.'

Kenny viewed his audience. He counted four yawns, two tears of boredom and one micro-sleep. He decided to push on regardless.

'The billionaires in the mining, weapons, agriculture, medicine, banking, energy and social media buy Earthling politicians and dictate the laws.

If we don't stop them, the Earth will face ecological collapse, social upheaval and potentially nuclear war. Without our help, this will likely happen before they get their shit together and become dignified members of our galactic society.'

The ensigns stared back at him with the same enthusiasm as goats looking at a hat.

'I also know that being trigennials, none of you care. So I'll get to the point,' Kenny told them.

The ensigns clapped, and Alicia joined them.

'Very fucking funny!' Kenny finally snapped. 'Alicia. Do you want to take a swing at this?'

She stood up and glared at the trigennials. At six-foot two-inches tall in her brand-new space pumps, she was an imposing sight.

'Unlike our dear sweet Commander Kenny, I am a heartless bitch and incapable of bullshit. So shut up and listen.' Alicia stared at them. 'We are putting together a small team to go down to the surface to become political consultants.'

'Which country?' Amanda asked.

'That choice was easy,' Alicia stated. 'We need a country that influences the rest of the planet. One with a system of government that is fully corrupt and twisted beyond comprehension. One where the political environment is one hundred percent driven by money, and money alone. A country where built-in gerrymandering ensures the majority is completely misrepresented and the government is hijacked by the goat-fucking minority.'

'Ye Gods! The United States!' Rebekah cried. She had always wanted to run amok in the US.

Her All-About-Me profile page describes Rebekah as a tall redhead with a body that could make a Hyperian mountain monk break his one-thousand-year vow of zero-masturbation. Everyone in the galaxy knows the All-About-Me site is packed with profiles of photo-shopped wannabes. In Rebecca's case, the monk story was real.

The now masturbating monk can be seen ripping the top off it all over town, including the local BallsMart sporting goods store.

'Well done, Rebekah! You get a star,' Kenny told her warmly. He pulled out his star roll, licked the back of one, plastering it firmly on her forehead.

Rebekah loved getting stars and made a super-big smiley face for Kenny.

Alicia sighed, hating Rebecca with renewed passion. She took a deep breath and painted the broad strokes of the plan. She angrily answered their stupid questions, then yelled at them some more. Not quite done, she insulted their collective intelligence and called into question the breeding of Kyle and Amanda.

'Brilliant start, people!' Kenny beamed proudly at his team. 'Who wants to go?'

Amanda, Rebekah and Kyle shot their arms up. The whole idea of messing with the Earthlings and being on TV sounded like fun in the extreme.

'Oh, fuck a Jakterian lizard! I'm not taking all three of you monkeys.' Alicia cried.

'Done!' Kenny said. 'We're all going!'

Alicia spat into her coffee cup, while Kenny became more and more excited.

'We have shit loads of work to do,' he told them. 'You will all get Earth identities. Our operations teams will abduct several well-connected political operatives, politicians and federal election committee legislators, or FECALs, as they are known as on Earth. We will brain-transfer them to create our back-stories, references and permission documents. Then we get to set up our election fundraising super packs.'

Kenny gave them a moment to digest this.

'We'll be spending money like the ignored first wife of an Yilliantian lopia-carbonate whore-hoarding mining baron,' he added.

The team realised at once that was a lot of money and became very excited.

'Where's all the money coming from?' Rebecca asked.

'Alicia will be hacking a few well-chosen financial institutions,' Kenny told her.

'How come Alicia gets to hack the money? I can hack money!' Ensign Amanda cried.

'Shut up, Amanda!' Alicia yelled. 'Or I'll transfer you back to the dead marine-paste processing factory where your mother conceived you during her five-minute fluid break while being train-fucked by nine of the ugliest Pistorise fisherman that shithole of a planet tried to drown in a bucket in a failed attempt to improve their gene pool.'

Amanda made a frowny-face. It was true that her mother was a nine-at-a-timer, but we all have needs.

'Okay, good! Alicia! What have I forgotten?' Kenny was now over-excited and started speaking way too loudly.

'Take it down a notch, Kenny,' Alicia told him, 'or I'll slap you.'

Kenny pondered that offer for a second, blushed, and took a breath.

'We meet again in the MIC (Mission Interface Centre) in one hour,' Kenny said, now slightly more subdued after Alicia's slap threat. 'Don't eat or drink anything. I won't be cleaning up three gut-loads of ensign-puke this time.'

One hour later...

The MIC technicians had harvested every scrap of available data on political consultant operations, including behaviours, beliefs and modus operandi.

At first glance, Kenny saw the data was truly horrific.

'Can this be right?' Kenny asked the technician.

'Yep. Political consultants are simply the worst people in our galaxy. They are almost as twisted as child-actor parents.'

'But the lying! The cheating! The complete disregard for the voters. So many lives ruined.' Kenny was worried. 'The money will come in handy though. Will you be able to erase all this shit after we return to the ship?'

'Nope,' the technician told him. 'This will be hard-wired in. We're not implanting memories here. These are core beliefs and reflexes. Your team will become arseholes from their pores to their balls forever.'

'You realise three of the team are women,' Kenny reminded him. 'They don't actually have balls.'

The technician paused and viewed Kenny. Remembering Kenny outranked him he edited his thoughts and formed a little smile.

'Thank you, Commander. I didn't realise that.' The technician's face reflected no sign of fatal irony. 'Although, I'm pretty sure Lieutenant Alicia once had junk.'

'Explains a lot,' Kenny conceded.

Kenny attempted to imagine life after the mission. Being back onboard the ship with a team of people who thought and acted as political consultants would be like living in a super-max prison, waiting to be shanked in the back or raped in the showers at any time.

Then he remembered that his tour would be almost over and they would become someone else's problem.

At any rate, he was just a soldier carrying out orders. Who was he to challenge the moral correctness of his superior's orders? That way leads to chaos, and he, Commander Kenny, future Captain Kenny, was not in the business of creating chaos.

At least not today.

Alien Activity Tracking Division — NORAD Aerial Tracking Station Colorado

'Is it over?' General Hans Kleene asked his number two guy, Colonel Jack Gustafson.

'Yes, sir,' Gustafson declared. 'The disk flew over Dallas for under an hour. Just long enough for everyone with a phone to shoot a video of it. It then went dark and left.'

'Better scramble some jets and drop flares. That can be our bullshit story for the press,' the general instructed. He hated these obnoxious aliens. They flew into his air space, zipped around, buzzed his cities, then disappeared.

For years, the General sent up fighter jets to intercept them, but the UFOs flew circles around his pilots. If they attempted missile lock, the UFOs simply disabled their systems.

The general remembered the time he ordered a pilot to fire his cannon at them. But that ended in tears when the UFO shut down the entire plane and it crashed in a field.

Today, they do none of these things. It's too traumatic for the pilots and the risk of death or injury is simply not worth it. But what really gets the general's goat, was the fact he had to lie. His job was to make thousands of normal people look like idiots.

How many times must he say, "No, you didn't see a huge disk hovering a hundred feet above your head. It was a weather balloon. It was swamp gas. Or it was Venus."

'How long are they going to keep doing this?' Colonel Jack asked the general. 'Can't they just get it over with and land? Pop the hatch and say hi?'

'Oh, fuck me, Jack! I don't know. Until they get bored, I guess,' the General was sick to death of answering that same old stupid question.

A few days later, on the monitoring floor one level below, a red light flashed.

'Looks like we have another ship,' Colonel Jack told the General.

The two men watched the tracking screen as an unknown craft entered the atmosphere above the northeast sector.

'A smaller one this time. Heading for New York?' Jack ventured.

'Or Washington. Better alert White House security and scramble some jets. The president screams his head off when we don't react,' the general said in a flat tone.

As the two men watched, the craft vanished from their radar screens.

'I'm getting some coffee. Then I'm going to hide in my office and read a boating magazine. Can you write the report, and make it sound like we have some level of authority over this crap?'

'Copy, General.' Colonel Jack replied.

Like the general, he too was over the whole UFO thing. He hated the fact they were too fast and elusive to shoot down.

Almost every day, Jack was reminded of the coyote and the road runner. He lived for the day these pestky aliens made one little mistake so he could finally kill one.

Colonel Jack watched the tracking screen for a few more seconds, but the alien craft failed to reappear.

'Not a buzz ship today,' he mused. 'Just another unknown visit to Earth for you fellas, hey?'

The ship the general and Jack were watching was Commander Kenny's forty-foot oblong-shaped transporter. Nothing flash, basically a space uber. The ship raced through the atmosphere and floated down toward the small town of Eltman, West Virginia.

The mission plan called for a period of Earth acclimatisation. While Kenny's observation team were experts at "watching" Earth, they had exactly zero hours "living" on Earth and interacting with Earthlings.

As the great galactic explorer and lover of all things fish, Sir Gleet d'Frome, taught them, there's a big difference between knowledge and knowing. D'frome often used this line at parties, hoping it would impress the ladies. Sadly for D'frome, it didn't work as often as you may think.

Nobody on Kenny's team knew what D'frome's bullshit meant. But it sounded really, really, smart.

In following the D'fromeian theory, the team was embarking on an acclimatisation road trip from Eltan, West Virginia to Washington, DC. During the trip they would be interacting with the Earthlings: learning their idiosyncrasies, eating the local food, and generally trying not to look too weird doing it.

The space uber circled around for a while and picked an uninhabited spot to land. The pilot activated his thermal cameras and found nothing but livestock.

'Happy with this, Commander?' he asked Kenny.

'Looks crappy enough. Put us down.'

Kenny's team was dressed as hikers. As they had some hiking to do, this seemed logical. All they carried were backpacks, some electronic stuff, lots of money and their newly created documentation.

Amanda insisted on taking her favourite toy. It was a stuffed Xzenian huffer rabbit that farted and pissed itself every time you rubbed it. Amanda found the bunny very comforting, and suffered crippling bouts of anxiety when separated from it.

The ship sat down on a patch of grass in the middle of a tree grove. Without their usual games of grab-arse, the team quickly disembarked. Then, without the need for ceremony, the ship climbed clear of the trees and vanished in a streak of bright light.

'It begins,' Kenny told Alicia. He'd been practising something cool to say for a few hours.

Alicia ignored him, more concerned with the fit of her hiker clothes.

'My fucking bra is too tight,' she grumbled. 'How do Earthlings wear this shit all day?'

Kenny checked her boobs. 'They look okay to me.'

'Pervert,' she told him.

'Whatever. Come on, people! We have a little walk ahead of us.'

Amanda's bunny rubbed against the inside of her backpack and farted.

It took the team an Earth-hour to reach the town of Eltman, and it did not disappoint.

In real life, the town was as shitty as the briefing images: old unpainted buildings, and those were the ones not boarded up.

The group of five, now technically classified as aliens, walked down the main street smiling and nodding to the locals they encountered. The locals stared at them for a second or two, then snarled back in return. All they saw were six foot tall, excessively pretty, city yuppies in expensive hiking clothes.

'They don't look very happy,' Amanda reported.

'Country folk are never happy and they hate city yuppies,' Kenny told her. 'Their Fox news tells them that all city people are communists and baby-killing democrats.'

'I know,' Amanda said. 'It's just really sad, is all.'

She rubbed her fart-rabbit for comfort.

Kenny spotted a local hotel adorned with a crud-stained sign that had lost all its ambition to attract customers since 1979. Through the crud, Kenny read: "Bar, Meals and Rooms".

Kenny smiled. *Perfect!*

'Now, people,' he began. 'We are political consultants. As such, we need to learn how to drink alcohol. When we reach Washington, there will be a lot of drinking and I don't want you making complete dicks of yourselves.'

The team considered this. They knew all about Earth-booze and were very keen to give it a nudge.

'Follow me and do as I do,' Kenny told them firmly.

Kenny marched them across the street until the blast of a car horn made him jump.

'Thank you, driver,' Kenny told the man with a big beard seated behind the wheel of a large American pickup truck. 'I'm okay!'

'Fuck you, stupid fucking tourist! Go back home!' the bearded man yelled.

Kenny went over to his window. 'I'm sorry, that's not possible right now. What's your name?'

The beard punched him in the face and drove off.

Alicia raced over and picked Kenny up.

'What the fuck was that?' Kenny asked.

'Didn't you read the briefing book? You don't talk to bearded hillbillies! What's wrong with you? I think I should lead from now on.'

'Fine,' Kenny moaned as Alicia swiped the blood off his mouth.

She turned to the rest of the group, who all had huge grins on their faces.

'Follow me,' she told them. 'Stop grinning or I'll punch you too.'

She took Kenny's arm and led him across the road. They found the hotel door and marched in.

'What a shithole,' Rebekah announced loudly.

Three old men, who appeared to be permanently attached to their bar stools, looked around.

'You got that right, sweetheart,' one of them said.

Alicia looked around, sizing up the room. She spotted a booth under a crud-stained window.

'Over here, people.' She directed them to the booth. They took their seats, not wanting to touch the table.

'I'll order drinks and food,' she told them.

'What's the food here?' Amanda asked.

'The food is whatever food I order,' Alicia declared.

Alicia went to the bar and waited. Then she waited a bit longer, until she began to wonder if she was doing something wrong.

'How do you get a drink here?' She asked one of the barflies.

'Good question, sweetheart. Old Harry is out back taking a dump,' he told her.

Taking a dump? Alicia considered this for a moment. *Oh, I know! Taking a shit*, she told herself.

'I normally take nine dumps a day,' she told the barfly. 'But long distance travel blocks me up.'

The three barflies stared at her dumbly. This was not the kind of information they were used to receiving. Especially not from a city tourist who looked like a supermodel.

Another minute passed.

'So, what's a group of folk like you doin' in a shithole like Eltman?' the barfly asked.

'We were hiking in the hills, now we're heading back to Washington,' Alicia said in her sweetest voice. It was fun practising Earthling communication skills.

'Washington, hey? Well good luck with that.'

'Thank you, sir. But luck is not on our agenda. Although, some gambling does sound like fun.' Alicia was very proud of herself. She was being very friendly and polite to the smelly old man.

The barfly, however, thought Alicia was very odd. But then, city folk were all odd.

Harry the barman finally emerged, wiping his hands on his apron.

'How can I help you?' he asked Alicia.

'We need a large jug of Long Island iced tea, please. And food for five people.'

'We don't make cocktails here, missy. But I can pour you a big jug of bourbon and coke. Singles or doubles?' he asked.

Alicia thought for a second. 'Better make it doubles. We need some serious drinking practice.' She nodded as she spoke.

The three barflies all turned to look at her again.

'This could be fun,' one said.

'My wife can cook you up some burgers and fries,' Harry offered.

'Perfect!' Alicia was getting excited.

Being in Eltman reminded Alicia of the time she went on a guided safari to the nether world of Jangto 7. It was an old mining town set up for tourism, where she got to sleep with three Krantian crystal miners in a tent. At least they told her they were miners, and she wasn't one hundred percent sure about the tent. Strange things happen when you inhale too much Krantian crystal. Anyhow, the trip was a real hoot. Real or not.

Armed with drinks, Alicia arrived back at the table to find Kenny had finally stopped bleeding.

'What in the name of Gort's great pants-puppet is that?' Rebekah asked.

'Bourbon and coke. It's sweet, you'll like it,' Alicia told her and offered a sickly smile.

'What about the food? I haven't eaten in three hours!' Rebekah cried.

'I swear to Gods, Rebekah. I'm about to slap you!' Alicia instantly lost her Earth-nice. 'Your food will be ready when it's ready.'

Five minutes later, the group had smashed down the first jug of bourbon and ordered a second.

'I'm gonna do some research with the locals,' Kenny announced, standing up too fast and wobbling. 'Hey, this Earth gravity is lighter than on the ship.'

'Sit down, Kenny,' Alicia warned him.

'Fuck nooo! I'm gonna mingle a mite,' Kenny told her and made his way, drink in hand, to the bar in what closely resembled a straight line.

He pulled up a pew and plonked himself down next to one of the barflies.

'So, what's it like living in Eltman?' Kenny asked one of the barflies.

'Living in Eltman? Are you fucking stupid?' the man asked him.

'Some people think I'm kind of stupid. Alicia thinks, well, I can't tell you what she thinks. She's a very rude girl,' Kenny told the man.

This made the barflies chuckle.

'Harry! Pour this man another drink,' the first barfly said. 'This is the most fun we've had for a while.'

Harry looked dubious, but did his job anyway.

'What do you do in Washington, son?' he asked Kenny.

'We're all political consultants,' Kenny told him, nodding with certain authority.

'And which party do you consult for? The Democrats?'

'No, sir! We are all staunch Republicans.' Kenny smiled and winked.

'I thought you had to be smart to be a Republican. You don't seem very smart to me.' The barfly didn't intend to insult, Kenny interpreted. It was just an observation.

'I've been told I'm very smart, just a bit goofy,' Kenny informed the man and winked again.

'Do you have something wrong with your eye, son? Do you have a twitch?'

'No, sir! A wink is an implied friend-centric, private information sharing gesture.' Kenny winked at him some more.

The barflies laughed again, for what Kenny saw was a very long time.

'I'm being rude,' Kenny announced. 'My name is Kenny.'

'I'm Huey. That's Louie, and the fella at the end is Dewy. As you can see, we have our ducks all lined up in a row.'

Huey, Louie and Dewy laughed again. This was a really big day for them.

Back on the *Mercurial Blue*, James monitored the mission live via the team's bio-communication sets. He could see and hear everything the team saw and heard. The feed was also being uplinked to the broadcast TV network and streamed in real time to around one trillion homes throughout the galaxy.

'Huey, Louie and Dewy are cartoon duck characters, Kenny. They're taking the piss,' James told him.

'I know that!' Kenny said out loud.

'What do you know, son?' Huey asked, his face wet with tears of laughter.

'Did your parents name you after ducks? That's nice. Does everyone in Eltman name their children after ducks?' Kenny asked, sending his new friends into further fits of laughter.

Needless to say, the TV ratings were going through the roof. The only person not happy was Colonel Hipu who was also watching the show on his big screen.

'Told you they'd make fools of us,' he said to Karen.

Karen took a break from her work, lifting her face out of the colonel's crotch.

'Think about the ratings,' she told him, spitting out a straggler hair. 'It's all about the ratings.'

At that moment, back on Earth, the hotel doors swung open and three mean-looking hillbillies marched in. They surveyed the scene and were more than a little surprised to see the five aliens in their favourite drinking hole.

'What in the name of green-eyed snake piss do we have here?' A man, wearing a faded Harley Davidson T-shirt that sagged at his skinny shoulders while lifting at the waist to reveal his pot belly, asked.

Alicia saw Kenny swing around on his bar stool and focus on the hillbillies.

'Oh, no,' she moaned.

'Howdy, partner!' Kenny yelled, before anyone could stop him.

'Oh, shit,' Huey whispered.

'What in the fuck-name of Jesus H Christ did you just call me?' The hillbilly yelled back.

One hundred million new galactic homes instantly tuned in. Word was out that *Reality Earth* was now the hottest show on galactic TV.

On the 400th floor of the Galactic Broadcast Network tower, Geon Plume and Todd Splick watched the rating numbers as they came in. They cried out in joy, and spontaneously formed a jerk-circle, furiously masturbating each other.

Kenny had virtually skulled his third glass of double bourbon. His world was now filled with rainbows, lollipops, and unicorns.

In this state of pure bliss, he had no capacity to foresee what was coming.

'I said, howdy, partner!' Kenny smiled at the hillbilly.

The hillbilly smiled back at Kenny, revealing two rows of yellow teeth that had sucked through more meth smoke than oxygen. He marched over to Kenny's chair and looked down at this grinning idiot in his brand-new designer fashion hiking gear.

At once, the hillbilly became confused. Something was very wrong. Why wasn't this city-pussy scared? It was like when a killer dog charged its prey, and the prey just sits there.

Fortunately for the hillbilly, his meth-brain took over and he raised his fist to hit Kenny.

But he was too slow.

Alicia had launched herself across the floor in one bound and punched the hillbilly in the back of the head.

Alicia's Seabertian highland giant goth meat-eating genes were similar to Kenny's tree dwelling fruit-eating genes, with one small difference: Alicia's genes made her smarter, stronger and way faster than Kenny.

She had also ticked the Assault Pioneer Ranger training box at the space academy, where she had learned all manner of exotic methods for hurting people.

When people asked her how she ended up on an observation ship, Alicia told them to go fuck themselves.

Yet, the rumours persisted that she had fornicated with her entire assault team, half of them being men, rendering them useless for combat.

This tragic event reduced the Ranger Corps' operational status to non-combatant for several months. They quietly transferred Alicia to Earth with the strict warning to never speak of it.

Alicia stood in the centre of the hotel floor over the comatose body of the previously very rowdy hillbilly. His two fear-struck buddies had already mustered the wit to not move or speak.

'Flee, drink or die,' Alicia offered her menu of options to the two upright hillbillies.

'Er, mind if we drink, ma'am?' They looked at their friend on the floor again.

Alicia smiled sweetly and nodded. The hillbillies walked around their friend and sat quietly at the bar.

Amanda, Rebekah and Kylie, still in their booth, all clapped.

'Now, where were we?' Kenny asked Huey.

Huey had stopped laughing at this point and stared back at Kenny with his mouth slightly opened.

'Don't catch a fly now,' Kenny offered, using his finger to close the man's mouth. 'Let's get down to business. How can the Republican Party make your life better?'

Alicia rushed over and grabbed Kenny by the arm.

'No time for that, Kenny,' she said, pulling him to his feet. She then addressed the bar. 'Can anyone sell me a car for twenty thousand dollars?'

'You can have my piece of shit, ma'am,' one of the hillbillies offered with near-meth enthusiasm.

Alicia took out the cash from her money belt. The documents department said it should be dry by now, just don't rub it too hard.

She handed the cash to the hillbilly, and he handed her a set of keys attached to a large medallion of a naked girl holding an assault rifle.

'Is that your girlfriend?' Kenny asked.

'I fuckin' wish, mister,' the hillbilly replied.

Five minutes later, strapped into their twenty-year-old, rust-infested F-150 pickup, the five aliens were heading north on the 231.

Kenny was in the back seat sound asleep and snoring well before they reached the 707-east turn-off. It had been a big day for him and he was very tired.

'I'm still hungry. Now I've got Kenny's head on my shoulder snoring and drooling,' Rebekah complained.

'Shut up, Rebekah, and don't fucking wake him or I'll put you out in the tray,' Alicia told her.

Rebekah did a big frowny face.

***

Geon Plume and Todd Splick had finished jerking each other off and lit large, Dalerian hand-rolled cigars. Each cigar cost about the same as a small car on Earth. That's because Dalerians have a severe allergic sensitivity to nicotine and within twenty seconds of hand-rolling each cigar, the Dalerian died. This process was very expensive in HR administration costs, but on the upside, Dalerian funerals were cheap as the cremation ovens never needed heating up.

The Galactic Humanoid Rights Organisation didn't really complain as Dalerians died early anyway. They all had terrible road-sense.

As Plume, Splick, and the rest of the galaxy watched, the Seabertian aliens travelled along the 707, then took the road to Salem and the 522.

'Can we stop at Salem and get something to eat?' Rebekah asked.

'We'll only stop if there's a restaurant,' Alicia told her. 'But no witches! Those fuckers are mean and I don't want to be turned into a toad.'

The three ensigns glanced at her. It appeared Alicia was losing her shit.

'You have the wrong Salem there, Alicia.' Kyle tried to help. 'We're in Virginia.'

'Don't tell me about Salem!' She snapped back at him. 'I know my witches.'

Kyle nodded. He couldn't argue with that.

Kenny was still blissfully asleep when the F-150 hit a pothole, causing Amanda's rabbit to fart and piss itself.

'Hey! What the…' Kenny cried. 'Where are Huey, Louie and Dewy?'

Alicia reached back and slapped him. 'Don't you cry, or I swear to Gods…'

She pulled the old truck into the McDonald's carpark.

'Food only. Don't engage with the locals,' she instructed them. 'Especially you, Kenny.'

Alicia got everyone settled at a table and went to order. The food menu looked amazing, with huge burgers bursting with salad crammed between perfectly cooked buns. They also offered golden fries and exotic drinks as big as footballs.

'Can I take your order?' The McDonald's server asked Alicia.

'I'll order twenty big macs, all with large fries and apple pies, please,' Alicia announced, then smiled at the server who's name tag that identified her as Destiny.

'Can I have a name for that order?' Destiny asked.

'Of course, Destiny. It's for Alicia,' she replied with another broad smile. 'When your mother named you Destiny, was she being ironic? Or did she believe your destiny was working in the fast-food industry?'

Destiny didn't know what "ironic" meant, but sensed she had just been insulted by the six-foot hiker-barbie bitch standing in front of her.

Destiny also knew she couldn't tell Alicia to fuck off, as this was her third job in five months and she was pushing her luck.

Destiny did, however, pick her moment for revenge. When the food came out, she managed to form a huge loogie and dropped it into a burger. She replaced the bun and wrapped it up tight. Using her favourite pen covered in glitter and stars, she wrote the name "Alicia" on it.

Back at their table, the aliens unwrapped their burgers and looked at them, then looked up at the menu board. The images on the board bore no resemblance whatsoever to the food in front of them.

'Typical Earthling bullshit,' Kyle told them, shrugged, and started eating.

'Did everyone get that special slimy sauce on your burgers?' Alicia asked.

They all checked and shook their heads.

'Ha, ha,' Alicia told them. 'You lose! I must be special.'

Twenty minutes later they were done eating and got back into the F-150. Not long after that they entered the town of Culpeper.

'Can we stop at McDonald's again?' Amanda asked. 'I need to give them back their food.'

They all agreed. A good puke was much needed by everyone. Alicia wheeled the F-150 into their second McDonald's car parking lot that day, and the aliens marched through the restaurant toward the toilets.

The restaurant manager watched their procession and ran up to greet them.

'Sorry, folks, the toilets are for patrons only,' he told them.

'We are patrons,' Kenny informed the young man, who carried more facial acne than a Zorbian crack-whore. 'We just ate at McDonald's Salem, now we're giving it all back.'

As the young man opened his mouth to speak, Kenny puked on the floor.

The man jumped back, but failed to move in time as Kenny-puke landed on his legs and shoes.

The young man took a moment to consider all the life choices he had made to this point. As he stared down at the vomit, he knew he did not deserve this. He mentally scanned his list of options, but all of them ended with him fetching a mop and bucket.

As the young man slumped off, the five aliens puked themselves clear of all the Earthling junk food. When the heaving, coughing and tears of self-loathing stopped flowing, Kenny called a meeting.

He was now sober and feeling all commandery.

'You all stink like Biscratchian prison barge conjugal pleasure-goats,' Kenny told his team. 'We need to find a motel and get cleaned up. In the morning, we're buying new clothes and a high-class vehicle to take us to Washington.'

The team was exhausted after their first few hours on Earth and liked the sound of taking a long hot shower.

'What's our number one rule?' Alicia asked the team.

'Don't stand too close to Kenny after he eats,' Kyle offered.

'Oh, I know! Avoid hillbilly bars,' Amanda said.

'No!' Alicia told them. 'It's don't talk to the locals. Also, don't do the other things too.'

***

The Aliens woke to a perfect autumn day in the township of Culpeper. Rebecca and Amanda were the first ones up and went for a stroll through town.

'Look at all these cute little shops,' Rebecca commented. 'When all this is over, we should go shopping.'

'I've seen this on Earthling television,' Amanda said. 'They love buying houses and fill them with all this stuff. Then they get sick of the stuff, dump it and buy new stuff.'

Rebecca considered this concept for a few seconds. She had entered Star Core straight out of school and never actually lived in a house. Shared dormitories and tiny units were her only homes. This made her a little sad.

'It would be so weird living in a whole house of your own,' she said. 'What would do with all that space?'

'Yeah, fuck that,' Amanda told her. 'You'd have to clean the place, and I hate dust. I also hate washing, cleaning dishes, and well, you know, everything.'

The short moment of nostalgia was now lost for Rebecca and she sighed.

'Cheer up!' Amanda told her. 'I'll buy you a coffee. Isn't that what Earthlings do?'

They walked another block until they found a coffee shop. The Culpeper Coffee Emporium, a hanging sign told them.

'This looks right,' Amanda announced, and they went inside. 'Let me order for you.'

'Er, okay.' Rebecca suddenly became nervous.

'May I help you?' a middle-aged woman asked without an abundance of enthusiasm.

'Can I order two frappuccinos with one pump of caramel sauce. Two pumps white chocolate. Three pumps of cinnamon dolce syrup. A swirl of cream, and a shake of sprinkles, please.'

The middle-aged women named Kelly, who was once young thin, perky, and popular stared at Amanda with pure loathing.

Kelly had been forced to take this job a week previously because she was made redundant at her law firm of over twenty years. She discovered the senior partner had replaced her with a twenty-two-year-old Miss West Virginia beauty pageant finalist who couldn't type or use the telephone exchange.

Kelly had been up since five a.m., after a fitful, depression-laden stress sleep. She then drove halfway across the county to open this shithole café owned by a complete arsehole who treated his staff like slaves and stole half of their tips.

Now she had two hiker-barbies standing in front of her ordering some bullshit coffee she'd never heard of.

Kelly could feel her blood pressure rising as the battle for self-control ragged inside her. At once, she knew she had lost the fight.

'What the fuck did you just order?' Kelly asked.

'Two frappuccinos with one pump of caramel sauce. Two pumps white chocolate. Three pumps of cinnamon dolce syrup. A swirl of cream, and a shake of sprinkles,' Amanda repeated and sighed to show her disapproval of Kelly.

In retrospect, Kelly knew it was the sigh that did it. She nodded and went to work on the order.

But Kelly didn't make frappuccinos. She made two iced coffees in take-out cups and thew them at the aliens, first Amanda, then Rebecca. Kelly's aim was true and she nailed both aliens with a full load.

'Enjoy your frappuccinos, girls!' She told them, laughing hysterically.

'Is this how the Earthlings drink coffee on TV?' Rebecca asked.

'Not really,' Amanda told her with milky coffee dripping off her face.

Later that day, Kenny and Alicia drove the old F-150 to Honest Tom's Car Emporium. They were wearing the very fetching outfits they found in a huge Earthling store called Walmart.

Kenny's T-shirt told the world how much he loved fishing, beer and scratching his nuts, while his tiny football shorts really made his blue eyes pop.

Alicia went for a more traditional look. She bought a tiny white-lace dress and no bra. She loved the way it let all the light and air through.

Kenny thought her huge black army boots spoilt the look, yet the local men seemed to disagree, based on the strange sounds and whistles they made when Alicia walked past.

In the car lot, Tom greeted the couple as they entered. As a church-going West Virginian car salesman, Tom was your quintessential conman and pervert. He viewed Alicia and Kenny with duelling emotions. Alicia made his heart pound and filled his mind with southern-fried filth, while Kenny just looked like a walking pile of easy money.

'Welcome to Honest Tom's!' He told them. 'How may I help you lovely folks today?'

Being a wise old pervert, Tom had long mastered the art of looking at women in micro-glances. He knew how to glance, absorb, quickly burn the image to memory, then look away.

He called this technique the "Y'all" method of perversion. 'Y'all better not get caught staring,' he boasted to his fellow church members.

'We need a car that will impress people in Washington city, Tom,' Kenny told him.

Tom nodded solemnly, working hard on this challenge. 'How much do y'all want to spend?'

Alicia pulled out multiple wads of hundred-dollar bills from her bright blue plastic Walmart handbag. She wanted the one with little rainbows stamped on it.

'Will this be enough, Tom?' she asked.

Being an old poker player, Honest Tom didn't smile or form a drop of sweat. But under his shirt, his heart was racing.

'I'm not sure,' he began, shaking his head. 'I do have a little German car that just arrived this morning. I mean, if you are looking for a car that will really impress, folks. Now, I have to say, I've had a lot interest in her already, but you seem like a real nice couple. Come on, I'll show you.'

Kenny and Alicia fell in love with the car at first sight.

Thirty minutes later, they pulled up at the motel in their 1989 sun damaged, sky blue, base model 911 Porsche. The engine ran on and spluttered a bit after Kenny shut it down, but Tom said that was normal. He also said the spongy brakes and cranky gearbox gave the car an authentic charm.

Kyle viewed the car and smacked his forehead. He was an Earth-car enthusiast and expressed his thoughts along the lines of, 'What the fuck are we going to do with that heap of shit?'

'You trigennials are so negative,' Kenny told him. 'This car is authentic! We know this because Tom said it is.'

Kyle smacked his head again.

'Let's try the food thing again. Then we'll hit the road to Washington.' Kenny was getting really excited.

'The guy at the motel said Arby's restaurants are the very best,' Amanda suggested.

'Arby's it is!' Kenny said.

With everyone clean, slept and dressed in their best Walmart outfits, the five aliens were ready to find an Arby's.

'How are we getting there?' Rebekah asked.

Kenny pointed to the tiny car.

'Oh, kill me now!' she moaned.

Alicia grabbed her by the hair and started pulling it. Kenny needed all his strength to release her grip.

The motel gardener stopped work and viewed the five aliens and their Porsche. He was then treated to what he later described as the best game of twister ever, as three very hot women and two goofy guys squeezed themselves into the tiny car.

***

Geon Plume turned to Todd Splick.

'Come on, seriously? Are they really this stupid, or are they actors?' he asked.

Todd Splick smiled. 'They are the cream of the Galactic Star Core, my friend, and one hundred percent authentic.'

'You're not trying to sell me an old Porsche now, are you?' Geon loved mixing his metaphors.

'You are a cheeky devil! Want some more olikian coffee?' Todd asked him.

'No way! My jaw still hurts after the last cup.'

***

The aliens ate their Arby's, puked it back up, and drove on to Springfield just south of Washington, DC.

The mission plan was to buy Washington-style political clothes and get serious political haircuts. Being genetically enhanced, tall and pretty, new clothes and cool hairstyles were easy to come by.

Kenny finally conceded he had made a mistake in buying the small car as it was completely impractical. Putting aside all sense of ego, dignity and personal pride, the aliens paid cash for a purple minivan.

Kenny assigned Kyle the duty of vehicular acquisition, as he kept banging on about how much he knew about cars. Kyle smiled confidently and told the team he had it.

Alicia rolled her eyes. She thought Kyle was a snooty little twat whose balls had not yet fully descended, making his voice high and squeaky.

In return, Kyle thought Alicia was an old lady who suffered severe Karen syndrome. Even though Alicia was only five years older than him.

Kyle was an amateur student of galactic anthropology. As such, he knew the Earthlings believed they had invented Karen syndrome. Yet, in reality, the syndrome was first identified almost one million years earlier after the first shopping mall opened on the planet of Zetron Nine in the Lorpe system.

It was there, during a seemingly normal Thursday late night shopping evening, a man accidentally bumped his shopping trolley into a cart owned by a Karen who went completely apeshit.

Karen indulged in her rage with such abandoned passion, it morphed into a full psychotic break from reality. Legend has it that the police had to taser her three times before she went down.

But even in her deeply shocked state, she managed to bite one cop and tear the finger off a second.

Kenny was oblivious to how Kyle saw Alicia, or how Alicia saw Kyle. And if he did, it was extremely unlikely he would have given a toss.

It had been a very exhausting few days acclimatising to Earth, and the aliens knew they needed another good night's sleep.

'Tonight, we'll stay in a hotel and be fresh for our arrival in Washington, DC tomorrow,' Kenny told them enthusiastically.

He winked at Kyle, who went to work tapping on his tablet screen. Within seconds he found them a hotel called the Best Western.

'Perfect!' Kenny told him. 'With a name like that, it must be the best.'

At seven p.m. the aliens met up in the motel restaurant.

They were showered and shaved, adorned in their new political consultant suits. Their appearance greatly impressed the Best Western staff who fawned over them profusely.

Their waitress was an excessively happy and friendly lady called Sharon. She was very proud to have a table of refined, good-looking people to serve. Her traditional clientele looked like other people's uncles that smelt like old horse.

Once again, ordering food became a nerve-racking experience. That said, and without any rational cause, they were feeling somewhat more confident.

'I'll have a go at this!' Kenny told them. 'Nachos for everyone and a huge pitcher of margaritas, please.'

The aliens looked at each other and shrugged. This was going to be either a great success, or a complete disaster. It could go either way.

Their fears were moderately belayed when the food arrived.

Placed before them was a magnificent spread of corn chips covered in melted cheese. There was red sauce infused with grey-coloured minced meat, strips of other red things. Sharon then topped everything with spoonsful of white goo.

Confusion set in.

'How do we eat this?' Rebekah asked.

'With your fingers, darlin',' Sharon told her. 'Or you can use a fork.'

They all looked back at the food and shrugged. One by one they stuck their fingers into the sticky mass and shovelled it into their mouths.

The restaurant was busy and the other guests enjoyed watching five well-dressed business people as they caked their faces in red sauce, sour cream and cheese.

The aliens wolfed down the first jug of margaritas, then ordered a second.

'Bless my bleached arsehole, that was good,' Alicia told them and belched like a deckhand.

The aliens demolished the nachos, burped a few times, then wiped their hands and faces.

To finish the night out, Kenny led his team in an old-world galactic folk song written eons ago on the forest moon of Chide. The Chidenese were a tragic people who, through no fault of their own, were born with three nipples. Needless to say, the infantile cretons who inhabited that solar system, notably the Norks, took the piss to no end.

This endless piss-taking caused the Chidenese people to suffer one of two anxiety-related mental conditions. They either became shy introverts, or homicidal narcissists, and not much in between.

Every full moon, the homicidal narcissist Chidenese travelled to the land of the Nork and cut off several pairs of Nork-balls. The balls were returned to Chide and stuffed with foam to make stress-balls for their introverted cousins. This horrific episode in Galactic history was later converted to a children's nursery rhyme to educate the young in the dangers of making fun of people who are different than themselves.

Especially those with three nipples.

With the singing done and the last pitcher of margaritas drank, the now drunk and repleted aliens sat quietly as their stomachs worked on the process of nacho-digestion.

In the quiet and peaceful moment, Kenny lifted his leg and farted. Unfortunately, he was leaning against Alicia who punched him hard in the arm.

'Don't cry!' she warned him.

With the fun over, Alicia gave Sharon a cash tip and thanked her for her service. Sharon wanted to tell Alicia that was normally reserved for soldiers, but the tip was so huge Sharon had a hot flush and nearly passed out.

She then asked the aliens for a selfie that she posted straight to her Facebook page.

On their way past reception, the manager whose nametag announced her as Maggie, came out to greet them.

'Oh, no!' she cried. 'What happened to your clothes?'

'Kenny ordered nachos,' Alicia told her.

'Well that just won't do! We have an overnight dry-cleaning service,' Maggie told them. 'If you give them to me, they'll be cleaned by the morning.'

Before Maggie could stop them, the five aliens stripped off down to their underwear and handed over their spoiled suits.

Maggie was now too stunned to speak. What started as a normal Friday night, had ended in five near-naked underwear models standing in her foyer.

Maggie knew at once this was not a Best Western best-practice procedure.

As guests walked past, husbands stared while wives slapped them. *Worth it*, the men judged. Children pointed and giggled, while mothers searched for plausible explanations.

'Okay, then.' Maggie had recovered. 'Let's get y'all covered up.'

She raced into the back room of the reception and grabbed five robes.

'Here y'all are! Put these on.'

It took the aliens a few seconds to work the robes out. Yet, in time, they got it.

'Mine's too small,' Rebekah moaned.

'No, it isn't,' Kyle told her and winked at Kenny. Kenny formed a grin that was instantly killed by Alicia who punched him again.

The Rise of Earl

The Harvard Finals Club president was a young man named Joshua Dolman-Hughes, who on this night, viewed his minions and smiled.

The twenty-two-year-old Dolman-Hughes oozed a self-righteous confidence that could only emanate from a person born in a world where literally everything was not only possible, but handed to you on an ornate fifteenth century silver tray.

Dolman-Hughes represented the latest batch of uber-privileged parasitical larvae to spawn from the dung heap of the American ruling class.

He and his classmates laugh when told America was a classless society.

Dolamn-Huhes knew there was the under-classes and the homeless who rarely travelled. The working poor who flew economy. The middle-class who flew economy premium. The working wealthy who flew business and maybe first class, if they could get a free upgrade.

Then, at the very top, were these snot-filled, degenerates who flew private. They were the sons of America's tsars and oligarchs.

'Welcome, gentlemen!' Joshua Dolman-Hughes greeted his people. 'Tonight, we party like kings! We will drink and fornicate like our forefathers, and let no man disgrace our great traditions with any of that woke, snowflake shit the other piss-poor universities must endure.'

Cheers broke out around the room. Feet stomped the hallowed hardwood floors, and a chorus of guttural chanting rose up. Amongst the boys whose balls had not yet fully descended, high-pitched squealing echoed off the walls.

The contract waiting staff hired for this night of debauchery stood in the shadows watching in dread. Each of them questioned their decision in taking this gig.

They rationalised it by remembering the hourly pay rate, and would do their best to smile while serving these young animals strong liquor until they became unconscious or puked, or both.

Then the bus arrived.

It was crammed with young debutantes all looking to hook-up with Harvard boys. Lex Timerson raced to the front of the reception line to cherry pick his party girl for the night.

The waiting staff supervisor reminded his team they had all signed non-disclosure agreements, and they were to forget everything they were about to see. This was easier said than done, they knew. The spectacle of smart, beautiful young women volunteering to become sexual playthings for a room full of America's future sociopaths was to be an horrific sight.

Lex Timerson was the last male child born to the legendary Timerson oil dynasty, where from the age of five, he was inducted into the family business.

Lex learned oil from his daddy, who learned it from his daddy, a man whose name sent tremors of fear into the hearts of anyone unlucky enough to encounter this tearaway rogue.

Thousands would come to dread the name Callous Tiberius Timerson.

Callous was, like most self-made billionaires, a pure narcissist in every concept of the term. He killed native Americans where he found them. He lied to, then robbed, countless poor dirt-farmers out of their tiny holdings. He corrupted elected officials, falsified mining leases, and murdered anyone who would not capitulate to him.

In his leisure time, Callous spent more time in gambling and whore houses than a Nevada gaming commissioner.

Callous discovered early in life that theft, Earth-rape and political corruption were the very cornerstones for American business success.

Over the generations, these lessons were passed down through the Timerson dynasty. The family skills were honed and perfected, the way a jeweller may work a rough stone on a cutting wheel, grinding off a little here and a little there, until a perfect arsehole-shaped diamond was formed.

In his late teens and early twenties, Lex was known by everyone who had the misfortune to encounter him as the prick's-prick. Even his mother, a woman who had seen more generational raw effluent than an itinerate pig farmer, failed to hide her dismay for the boy.

As she watched him mature, she knew Lex to be a drunk and an Old Testament version of an idiot. In contemporary terms, the boy was a complete waste of space. He drew in oxygen from one end and excreted disappointment and family embarrassment from the other.

Despite all this, being the eldest Timerson male, he was next in line to be king.

They sent him to the Harvard School WASP drinking club, where Timerson senior sent a huge cheque every year. This vast sum of money ensured his lazy, moronic son graduated with an MBA.

In the following years, and to no one's great surprise, young Lex made a complete balls-up of every venture penetrated with his pointy little nose.

After countless scrapes with the law, the IRS and bankruptcy court, the Republican Party decided Lex Timerson would become the next governor of Texas. As the people of Texas only ever voted Republican, they had no choice.

This was one job he did well. Lex went hunting and fishing, leaving the actual job of governing to his daddy's pals. On the one day each week Lex went to work, he signed every piece of pro-Republican legislation that passed his desk.

Being a completely unengaged individual, Lex became the favoured son of the GOP. So much so, GOP leadership decided he should become president of the United States.

What the GOP leadership failed to acknowledge was that the Republican voter had changed.

They didn't want the traditional Republican polished turd any more. They had tasted genuine lunacy, and they liked it.

In 2015, grass-roots Republican voters elected a multi-bankrupt businessman. A man who had been accused of fraud countless times, painted his face orange, and grabbed women by the pussy. A man so stupid, that he told the press when he was about to commit a crime, then went right ahead and did it. He did it multiple times, right there, on national TV.

The result of this new reality came to pass in the following presidential primaries. Their man, Lex Timerson, was handed his hat and shown directions to the bar.

Horrified by these events, the GOP knew drastic action was needed. They knew to survive as a political force, they had to get their crazy back.

This opened the door for the emergence of Team Kenny. From sources unknown, the GOP leadership all knew for a fact, Team Kenny was their only hope.

Republican Party HQ — Washington, DC

The assembled Republican strategists were waiting anxiously in the GOP executive boardroom.

To a person they looked a little worse for wear. Everyone had headaches and the light in the room was blindingly bright. Adding to their misery, for the first time in their lives, they did not want coffee.

These, of course, were all side-effects of being abducted by aliens and experiencing a brain transfer procedure.

The Seabertians used to call the process "brain washing" but that term seemed a little old-fashioned. Yet, having their "brains washed" was exactly what these people had endured.

It was a process of evacuating all the available electro-neuronic data from the host brain and storing it in digital form. The Seabertian super-computers erased selected memories and adding the desired new thought patterns.

As a result, the GOP executives believed Kenny and his team of aliens were first-rate political operatives, who were held in very high esteem in the political world.

In their minds, the decision was already made. Team Kenny was going to pick, groom and elect the next GOP president of the United States.

As they waited, the GOP people could not fathom why they didn't want coffee, and why sunlight was hurting their eyes.

'Close the curtains, Jeff,' Julia Reynolds said. 'My eyes are killing me.'

'Close them yourself,' Jeff Lasser told her, feeling quite murderous.

'Fuck me, Jeff! You're such a weasel-assed little cocksucker!' Julia yelled at him and pulled the curtain cord.

Everyone stopped working and stared at Julia. That seemed a little uncalled for, they mused. Julia was normally very nice. This was indeed a very strange day.

The door opened and an intern appeared.

'Team Kenny is here,' she announced.

'Thank God,' Lake Freedmen declared. He was getting sick of waiting and couldn't stop twitching. This was another side-effect of being dragged onto an alien spaceship at two a.m. and having sharp pins inserted into your head.

Kenny, Alicia, Amanda, Rebecca, and Kyle marched in looking like a million bucks. The nachos stains were dry-cleaned out of their suits, and their hair was perfect. The team was ready for business.

'Welcome!' Julia told them. 'Thank God y'all are here. We are looking forward to getting your advice.'

'Well, Julia, we look forward to helping out,' Alicia said, flashing her very best smiley face.

Everyone in the room smiled like idiots for a little longer than was strictly necessary.

'So, who have you got for us?' Kenny asked, breaking the awkward silence.

The GOP people glanced at each other nervously.

Lake Freedmen took the lead.

'As you know, GOP candidates must be perfectly matched to the personalities of Fox News viewers.'

'That's right, Lake,' Julia concurred. 'Each preferred GOP candidate must be uneducated, and I mean seriously uneducated. They must know nothing except for the news Facebook sends them, and the manic rantings on Fox News.'

The GOP people paused while Kenny took notes.

'They must know nothing about the rest of the world and less about history. Especially American history.' Jeff Lasser took up the slack. 'They must be terrified of foreigners and minorities, and they hate women. They also need to be ignorant of even the most basic concepts of economics, trade and commerce.'

'Thank you, Jeff. Have we forgotten anything?' Julia asked her team.

'I forgot the most important part,' Jeff Lasser told her. 'Republican voters call themselves Christians. Yet, unlike Jesus Christ himself, they are nearly all selfish, greedy and devoid of all empathy. They love politicians who are corrupt liars, and have a complete disregard for the health of the planet that their God built for them.'

'Well said, Jeff,' Julia told him. 'The key is that our winning candidate must never waver from the Fox News talking points, no matter how outright dishonest, illegal or morally corrupt these talking points may be.'

'Sounds right so far,' Kenny told them.

'As you know,' Lake continued, 'without our Fox News propaganda machine, GOP candidates could not get elected as a dog-catcher, even in Utah or Texas. The GOP has no social improvement or nation-building policies. We only care about giving everyone guns and tax-breaks for the rich.'

As they listened, the aliens, who were over three hundred thousand years more socially advanced than the Earthlings, felt ill.

'There is an upside,' Julia began. 'We are very keen on cutting spending to help the poor, and giving half of our national wealth to the military each year. Although we are not at war, the GOP demands America should have the most expensive military in the world.'

'In addition,' Lake Freedmen joined in, 'we are fully behind allowing everyone to own guns. Not just hunting rifles, but handguns and military assault rifles. This includes men charged with spousal abuse, the mentally ill, outlawed militias and everyone on the terrorist watchlist.'

The room was silent while they digested this litany of horror.

'So, in saying that, would you like to meet our candidates?' Julia asked brightly.

'Yes please!' Kenny told her with a huge smile. 'This is very exciting!'

The GOP people smiled nervously, while Rebekah, Amanda and Kyle clapped.

The intern flicked on her computer and the image of a fat-faced bearded man in a US flag-bearing, crud-stained baseball cap appeared on the big TV. He wore a blue pin-striped suit that was way too small and cut completely wrong for his ground-hog body type.

'Hi, folks! I'm Earl!' The man told the camera. 'I'm from Ken-tuck-ee, and I sells cars. I wants to become president of these United States 'cause I believes in freedom. We don'ts gots no freedom no more 'cause of them commie Democrat assholes. Now, I'm not sayin' we should use violence. But if those commie baby-killers come down here to my neck of the woods, well, let's just say, theys won'ts be gettin' out again.'

'Perfect!' Kenny said. 'Next!'

The following presentations went along a similar theme. Yet it was the selection of female candidates who really shook Kenny's confidence.

If the presentations went one second longer Alicia was ready to kill everyone in the room, then herself.

'I believe they all match the Fox News audience perfectly,' Kenny said joyfully. 'Give us a couple of days to study these tapes and do some preliminary vetting, and we'll get back to you.'

The GOP people were rapt. Having someone else make this horrendous decision for them was a Godsend.

***

Later that night a man who, if not for the right-wing political structure, would be lucky to get a job in the zoo cleaning up the monkey shit, was busy entertaining himself in his twenty-million-dollar home in Brooklyn.

Josh Garety was one of the leading Fox News fearmongers who, at that moment, was dressed as Batman with a leather belt fastened from his neck to the top of his bedroom door.

Garety was furiously masturbating his lightly wooded penis to a video starring his post-op transexual girlfriend shooting a rare white rhino in a Kenyan animal sanctuary. As he tugged, Garety lowered his weight until the belt around his neck became tighter, finally dumping his load on the floor.

With mixed emotions of euphoric gratification and dark self-loathing, Garety attempted to stand up. Unfortunately, he lost his footing on the slimy mess and fell back to the floor.

He was a squat, heavily built man, and what he lacked in upper body strength, he gained in a high BMI. This combination handicapped his efforts in successfully pushing himself to his feet.

All the while, the pressure from the belt around his neck prevented air from reaching his lungs. The more he squirmed in the puddle of his own mess, the weaker he became.

It was at that moment, Josh Garety realised he was going to die.

'Fuck my Gods!' Lieutenant Rick, the Seabertian abduction team leader, yelled as he entered the bedroom. 'Hey, boys, we've got another masturbating Republican dressed like Batman trying to hang himself. Why are they always dressed like Batman?' Lieutenant Rick asked no one in particular.

The Seabertians grabbed Garety and untied the neck-belt. As he did so, Garety began breathing again and regained consciousness.

'Hey! What the fuck's goin' on!' he screamed, viewing the Seabertians.

'Shut up, you idiot!' Sergeant Lisa yelled and kicked him hard in the balls.

Garety screamed, then bleated like an apoplectic rat-weasel, which was in fact his spirit animal.

'Was that entirely necessary?' Lieutenant Rick asked her.

'I wouldn't say it was necessary,' Lisa confessed.

Lieutenant Rick simply shook his head at her. Lisa kicked Garety again, purely out of spite.

Lieutenant Rick knew not to argue with Sergeant Lisa, as she was one hell of a good ball-kicker.

Rick flashed Garety with a stun phaser and the noise stopped. The team placed his limp mass into a silver bag and carried him out to the space uber parked in the backyard.

Fifteen minutes later, the transport reached its dock inside the *Mercurial Blue* and the team dumped Garety onto a hover gurney and floated him to the brain-transfer lab.

Garety was conscious again, yet paralysed, all except for his eyes, which swung wildly from side to side viewing the interior of the alien ship.

'The boys at the gun club are never going to believe this shit,' he whispered.

The brain-transfer technicians were ready for him and wasted no time inserting electrodes into his head.

'Can you shove a probe up his arse?' Sergeant Liza asked.

'This is a brain transfer. We stopped doing anal probes years ago,' the technician said. 'Besides, I'm not paid enough to go near his arse.'

Liza nodded. The man made a valid point.

'Fine then, I'll do it,' she told him.

The technician took a one step back and waved her forth. Lisa picked up one the larger probes and jammed it deep into Garety's arse.

'You forgot to use lube,' the technician told her.

'No, I didn't,' Lisa told him and smiled weirdly. The technician cringed and took one more step back from her.

Garety's brain data download only took a second as his mind was almost empty. It contained a few snippets from the Bible, some sporting statistics, a brief transsexual-sex highlight reel, and this week's GOP talking points.

'Last time I saw a brain this small was that one time you people had me do a squirrel,' the technician told Lieutenant Rick. 'What was the squirrel used for anyway?'

'Never mind,' Rick told him.

Garety's data was quickly edited and uploaded back into his brain. The latent new data would completely change Garety's view on the world. He would soon care about poor children and minorities, and be very keen on health care for all.

He would also become a champion for higher paid teachers, fully funded day-care, and investing in clean energy. Then his crusade against tax-avoiding billionaires would begin.

'This once completely corrupt arsehole is about to become an actual human being,' the technician declared with sense of pride.

'Did you install the delay code and the activation phrase?' Lieutenant Rick asked.

'Surely did,' the technician told him with a wink. '"Deck the hall with guns and ammo," right?'

'Great. Cheers for that,' Rick told him and returned the wink.

They both knew winking at each other was a Seabertian thing, but they didn't care.

Later that morning, Garety woke up in his bed with extremely sore balls and a weirdly gaping arsehole. He thought the arsehole thing was particularly odd, as he had recently stopped using his arse-dildo. The dildo, he called it Ralph, made his farts sound like elephant calls.

This sound amused his workmates, but was more than a little bit socially embarrassing, especially when he farted in church, or at his mother's nursing home.

Garety also had no interest in his morning coffee.

***

In the studios of Galacom, Todd Splick and Geon Plume lit another cigar as they watched the ratings bloom to unprecedented levels, then spread to the more enlightened parts of the galaxy. They realised *Reality Earth* had morphed from a straight comedy to become a comedy/drama.

'Wow!' Plume announced.

'Fucking wow!' Splick concurred. 'Did you know, and here's an interesting statistic; there have only been like two hundred planet-based reality shows in the last millennium that have crossed the comedy-drama bridge.'

Plume smiled at Splick. 'Have you got any more olikian?'

'You really are one randy little bastard,' Splick told him.

Geon Plume blushed and gave Splick a coy little smile, then his phone rang.

'Yes,' Plume answered. He listened for a while and said, 'I'm sure we can do that. It'll cost you one million Murks.'

Murk was the new galactic crypto currency that everyone in the advertising world was using. They loved it because it could zoom from world to world faster than the tax office could track it. Then it ended up in banks on the distant Bleek System where they spoke none of the known galactic languages.

'Can we get them to wear Sklock watches?' Geon asked Splick.

'New sponsor, hey?' Splick asked.

'A fat million Murks worth,' Geon confirmed.

Tod Spick hit his zipper.

***

Team Kenny spent the next day reviewing the presidential candidate videos wearing brand new Sklocks that were delivered by space uber overnight.

'My Sklock just told me that watching Republican Presidential candidate videos is very slimming,' Rebecca announced. 'These people are so nauseating , I will never eat again.'

Alicia, for the first time since Kenny had met her, was very quiet. Her new Sklock sensed her depression and told her she was very pretty.

'Thank you, Sklock,' Alicia told her watch. Sklock gave a her a sweet little I- love-you wrist vibration.

'Is this where America is right now?' Kyle asked. 'Will they actually run one of these people for president?'

'They've done it twice already,' Kenny said. 'Remember George W. And the orange ape?'

Kenny was right, Kyle knew, and fell into his own silent depression.

'You're handsome,' Kyle's Sklock told him.

'Shut the fuck up, Sklock,' Kyle yelled at his watch.

Sklock hated being yelled at, and began to cry.

Team Kenny watched this interaction and shook their heads at Kyle's poor form.

'People!' Kenny said. 'Can we focus, please'

'So, it's Earl then?' Amanda asked.

Team Kenny viewed each other and nodded sadly.

'It's Earl,' Kenny confirmed, and the next day they flew to Kentucky.

It was a big day, as the "Earl for President" campaign was about to kick off, and Kenny's long-time dream of helping the Earthlings would begin.

It was, however, the first time the aliens had passed through an airport. Much to their surprise, it all went swimmingly, except for Alicia, of course.

A young TSA man named Jed—short for Jethro—watched Alicia approach his security station and got an instant chub. Jed liked red meat, lifting weights and using his penis-pump, but only when his mum went out to the shops.

Jed also had plastic hairy nuts hanging from the tow ball on his pickup truck, and a sticker on the back window telling the world he hated fat chicks. In fact, apart from pumping up his penis, Jed only really liked three things: his truck, his guns and Jesus, of course.

'Hold your arms out, ma'am,' Jed told Alicia.

She stood and stared at the boy. He gave her the flappy-arms motion, and with repressed hostility Alicia copied him.

Jed waved the hand-held metal detector over her body, and on the way down he flashed it over his own watch.

'*Beep*,' the metal detector said.

'Are you wearing anything metal?'

'No,' Alicia said.

Jed waved the wand, hitting his watch again.

'Ma'am, I'll need you to remove your jacket.'

Kenny saw that Alicia was getting ready to hit the boy, so he moved in close to her.

'Be good now,' he whispered in her ear.

Now Alicia wanted to hit Kenny too.

'Ma'am, your jacket please,' Jed told her.

Alicia sighed and stripped off her jacket and Jed moaned softly. He hated his job, but every now and then God sent him a little gift.

Jed was on a roll and going for the prize: a full body scan. He waved the wand slowly over Alicia's body again and flashed his watch again.

This time Alicia saw him.

She pulled back her hair, leaned forward, and whispered something into the boy's ear. To this day no one knows what Alicia said. But whatever it was caused Jed's chub to vanish faster than a quick swim in the blue pond on the ice star of Viktaria.

The now physically shaken Jed waved Alicia through, while Rebekah, Amanda and Kyle clapped.

'Well done!' Kenny told her.

Alicia grinned at Kenny, then flicked up her wrist, hitting him in the ball-sac.

'You're a real deJong, Alicia,' he told her, wincing from his bent knee position.

'Thank you,' she smiled, showing him two rows of perfect, bright white teeth.

The GOP flew all their executives first class, and the aliens kept the flight attendant hopping the whole time.

'Warm nuts!' they yelled. 'More vodka!' they yelled some more. 'Moist towels!' they continued yelling.

Two hours and one frazzled flight attendant in need of a personal day later, their plane landed in Kentucky where they disembarked without incident.

'I'm hungry!' Amanda told them in her best whiny voice.

'Fuck me, Amanda!' Alicia told her. 'You just ate a pound of warm nuts on the plane.'

But they also knew if they didn't feed her, she'd be complaining all day.

'Hey look!' Kyle announced. 'A McDonald's!'

'No!' everyone yelled.

They found a meal of greasy Chinese delights that didn't make them excessively sick, then found a car hire kiosk.

'Can you rent us the most inbred, red-neck, gas guzzling truck you have, please?' Kenny requested from D'juna serving behind the counter. 'I imagine the D is silent?'

'Your D will be silent forever if you keep up with that shit,' D'juna told him.

'Fair enough,' Kenny told her.

Thirty minutes later the team, mounted in their bright red Ram truck, was on route to Earl's Executive Autos on the magic mile in one of Louisville's more dodgy suburbs. Alicia insisted on driving, as she was feeling all full of herself after the TSA incident and the good nut-flicking she gave Kenny.

She reached down and turned on the radio, just in time to hear Jonny Cash singing about a man he killed in Reno, just to watch him die.

'And you all call me a sociopath,' Alicia told them.

Team Kenny exchanged glances, but neither confirmed nor denied their opinion of Alicia. Instead, they sat quietly listening to the story about Folsum Prison, and the blues Jonny Cash experienced there after his rampage of murder.

Earl's car lot was easy to spot and Alicia wheeled the truck into the parking area next to the office.

The man they had travelled halfway across America to see, the shiny new hope of Republican politics, Earl himself, was busy making face-love to a super-sized hotdog with the lot.

He waddled out to greet them with half a dog in one hand and a face smeared in red and yellow sauce.

'Meet America's next president,' Alicia told them.

'They've had worse,' Rebekah said, and they all murmured in agreement.

Kenny jumped out of the truck. 'Earl!' he yelled.

Earl eyed the truck as it arrived. *Looks like the government*, he thought. To Earl, anyone he had not yet met in his life looked like the government.

'Who the fuck are you!' he demanded.

'We're the motherfuckers who is gonna make y'all president!' Kenny yelled back at him.

Alicia smacked her forehead. Rebekah, Amanda and Kylie did frowny faces.

Earl, however, farted and sharded in his pants.

'God fuckin' darn it,' he moaned. 'That's twice!'

After he had recovered what passed for redneck dignity, he invited Team Kenny into his conference office. The office was a rusty twenty-foot shipping container fitted out by his meth-head brother, Steve. The floor was carpeted with dumpster-reclaimed fake grass, and the walls were lined with mismatched sheets of reject plywood.

At night, Earl let guard dogs sleep there. The multiple layers of dog urine had morphed into an overpowering, slow release, gaseous surge.

Kyle was well known for suffering a heightened sensitivity to nearly all forms of urine vapour. Within seconds he became light-headed and began to hallucinate. Hillbilly ghosts began drifting out of the fake grass and he began to cry.

Amanda saw this and held him tightly.

'Suck your thumb, Kyle. It will help,' she told him. Alicia and Rebekah both watched this and took a full step back.

As Kyle sobbed, Earl took a large bite from his hot dog.

'Anywho,' Kenny said as his eyes burned, 'the GOP leadership was very impressed with your audition tape, and we have reviewed it.'

Earl tore his eyes away from Kyle sucking his thumb and focused on Kenny.

'What?' he asked.

'Your presidential candidate tape, Earl. The one you sent the GOP. We liked it!' Kenny told him.

'Oh yeah, the tape!' Earl was on it.

'Do you still want to be president, Earl? You know, of the U-nited-states of Murika?' Alicia jumped in. Her attention span was being tested and her eyes were dog-urine burning.

'Oh, yeah! Murika! Fuck yeah!' Earl told them enthusiastically.

'Brilliant!' Kenny smiled at him. 'Then we have a lot of work to do. The Republican National Convention is on in two weeks and it's our job to get you ready.'

Earl, having been on a strict diet of processed meats, highly enriched flour products, and bourbon for forty years, suffered chronic type two diabetes.

As such, it took a while for information to travel the distance between the clogged neuropathways from his ears to his brain. It then had to fight its way through a dense cloud of brain-fog and into his frontal lobe for processing.

The team stood and waited.

'Take a seat,' Earl offered them.

'No!' the aliens yelled in unison.

'We have you booked into the Sheraton Hotel downtown. Meet us there tomorrow morning at ten a.m. and we'll get started with your campaign,' Kenny announced.

Earl processed this then nodded furiously, grunting like a mountain pig.

'Leave your hot dog behind, please,' Alicia told him.

'Aww,' Earl looked down at his hot dog. He loved that dog, but reluctantly said, 'Yes, ma'am. I guess.'

The next morning, one full hour late, Earl arrived in the foyer of the hotel.

It was not a pretty sight.

'How are you feeling, Earl?' Kenny asked, trying to hide his disgust.

'Not great,' Earl grunted. 'My brother Steve came over with a bottle of Jack and we drank it. Then I found an old bottle of shine, and well, I guess we must have dranked it too.'

'Wonderful,' Kenny smiled, trying to hide his disgust. Then Earl's stench caught up with him. Kenny wavered, almost losing his footing.

'Okay, follow me.' He motioned Earl to walk with him to the elevators.

For a full fifteen seconds, Kenny endured the longest ride in the history of vertical travel. Earl stank like a pig that all the other pigs had used as a toilet.

The journey finally ended and the pair entered the hotel suite.

Kenny and Alicia decided to pull rank and ordered the ensigns to clean him up. The ensigns made huge frowny faces.

'Do it! Or I'll send you home,' Alicia told them.

The trigennials reluctantly went to work. They ran a bath and striped Earl naked. Amanda puked once and Kyle kept a thumb in his mouth the whole time.

They shoved the struggling Earl into the warm soapy water while he screamed, 'It ain'ts even bath day!'

It took some doing, but the ensigns managed to scrub layers of encrusted crud off Earl's body. They even managed to wash the grease out of his hair. Rebekah asked if they needed HAZMAT clearance before releasing the bathwater down the drain.

The team shrugged and pulled the plug away.

Now wearing his bleached-white Sheraton robe, Earl looked like a little fat, alcoholic, meth-Jesus.

'Earl!' Kenny said. 'You look like a million bucks. Now for your haircut.'

Earl viewed the lady hairdresser who was busy setting up her station without enthusiasm.

'But she's a girl!' Earl complained. 'Buck's the only one I trust to cut my hair.'

'Not today!' Alicia snapped at him, and shoved him down on a chair.

Earl didn't know if he was aroused or terrified. He looked toward Kenny for support.

Kenny simply shrugged at him and shook his head.

'Don't fight her, Earl,' Kenny warned him. 'She's stronger than both of us.'

After thirty minutes of hollering, buzz shaving and clipper work, the hairdresser asked for a shot of vodka and a cigarette.

Earl, on the other hand, looked almost human.

'Okay! We're almost there!' Kenny declared and clapped his hands.

On cue, a local tailor marched in.

'Don't give us any shit, Earl,' Alicia told him. 'You're being fitted for new suits.'

The tailor looked at Earl's body type and moaned. Nonetheless, like the professional he was, he went to work.

When he had taken all his measurements, the tailor promised the suits would be ready in two days. Alicia handed him another thousand dollars.

'I mean, tomorrow morning,' he told her.

She smiled at the man and patted his small, bald head.

Alicia then took Kenny by the arm and led him to one side.

'Time for the talk,' she told him. Kenny nodded and took a deep breath.

Earl looked like a man who had endured too many changes all at once. Clean skin. A new haircut by a woman with actual haircutting qualifications, and fitted for clothes only homosexual Democrats wore.

Worst of all, Earl was almost sober.

This was a new experience for him, as he had not been sober since he visited Las Vegas 1987. By all accounts, he bit a hooker who promptly became homicidal, chasing him all the way out of town and into the desert, where she left him for dead.

The now defeated and deflated Earl found himself a chair and sat. The man was a picture of pure misery.

'Can I go home now?' he asked in a hollow voice.

'No,' Kenny replied, pulling up another chair beside him. 'We need to talk about you becoming president,' he began.

'Uh huh,' Earl replied.

'There will be many changes in your life, Earl,' Kenny said.

'Uh huh,' Earl agreed, nodding like an old tired dog.

'You will need to stay in the hotel with us so we can get you ready for your political campaign. If you go home, you'll turn into a bush pig again. You don't want that, do you, Earl?'

Earl considered this. He didn't like being in the fancy hotel. It had hurt him. All that bathing and hair cutting. All he wanted was to go back to his dog-piss container office and get on the Jacks with his brother.

Alicia was ready for this new reality and had an intervention ready.

She reached into her wallet and held up a cheque for one million dollars. Earl saw that his name was on the check. He looked closer, viewing the bank hologram and embossed seal.

'Hey! That thing's fuckin' legitimate!' he told her.

Alicia nodded slowly.

'Well now, little lady!' Earl told her, discovering a new level of energy and enthusiasm. 'That's a whole different story, ain't it!'

Alicia smiled at him again, exposing her two rows of bright white teeth.

'If you want this cheque,' Alicia began, 'you need to do everything we say. If you give us any shit, Earl, I will burn it right in front of you. Then, I'll send you straight back down the piss-filled rat-hole where I found you.'

She took a step back and held up the cheque in one hand and a cigarette lighter in the other.

'What do you say, Earl?' Kenny asked.

Earl's blood-shot eyes were locked on the cheque while Alicia flicked the lighter to life and moved the flame slowly toward it.

'Don'ts burns my cheque! Yes! Yes! I'll do anything you says!' Earl was almost in tears.

'And no more bullshit?' Alicia asked, nearing the flame closer to the paper.

'No! No bullshit! I swears!' Earl yelled.

'Outstanding!' Kenny blew out the flame.

'Whew! That were a close one!' Earl told them.

'First up, you can't wear that robe all day,' Alicia told him. 'Put this on.'

She threw Earl a white onesie with "I Wants To Be President" embossed in red lettering.

'Perfect!' Kenny told them.

'Time to eat,' Alicia announced. 'Do you want a hotdog?'

'Yes, ma'am,' Earl replied and a long string of saliva dripped from his mouth.

'Oh, fuck me,' Alicia whispered.

Later that night they took Earl to the roof and waited for their space uber.

'Fuckin' cold up here in a onesie,' Earl complained.

The ship arrived in stealth mode and nobody saw it until it hovered right next to them.

'What the…' Earl screamed and almost fell over backward.

'I know, right!' Kenny told him, pulling Earl upright. 'Spooky!'

Kenny, Earl and Alicia all boarded the ship together and flew back to the *Mercurial Blue*, where Earl puked a few times along the way.

'Sorry, guys,' the pilot told them. 'I forgot the puke bags.'

On board the *Blue*, Kenny met with the brain transfer technician to discuss Earl's new brain data.

'Okay, I think we have everything,' the tech told Kenny. 'He now has a capacity to form complete sentences. He can recite all the key Republican talking points, including: guns, troops, no taxes for the rich, coal and Jesus.

'Yep, looks good.' Kenny read from the list. 'Hates free health care. Wants to increase spending on the military and fight more foreign wars. Cancel America's slave history being taught in schools. More Bible taught in schools. Round up Mexican children born in the US and send them back. More drilling for oil in Alaska and all the national parks.'

'Looks like a good start,' Alicia said. 'We can fill in the rest. We just need Earl to say "freedom" every chance he gets and tie it into anti-socialism rants.'

'Oh, there's one more thing,' Kenny said. 'We need him to lose thirty pounds in two weeks. From now on, Earl only eats leafy green vegetables and organic free-range chicken. He goes to the gym every day and hates alcohol and meth.'

The tech typed the request into his table. 'Leafy greens, chicken, gym, and no booze or meth. We're ready to go,' he told them.

Earl was strapped face-up on the transfer table, and was given a sedative to ease the stress of the transfer process.

'Don't fight it, Earl,' was the last thing he remembered Kenny telling him.

Two weeks later

The Republican National Convention was in full swing.

Speakers raged their hate for all things liberal spanning two whole days. Now, with the crowd fully fluffed-up, it was time for their keynote speaker, Earl.

The GOP had marketed Earl as the "Real American" man. He was coarse, crude and stupid. A man for the heartland, who could cut through Washington bullshit and get the deal done.

Kenny's team were rapt. They had completely transformed the man who was now walking on stage. Earl had dropped thirty pounds and achieved a near-humanoid body-shape. His tailor was also a happy man. As Earl continued to lose weight, the constant flow of new suit orders made him a rich man.

With his new addiction to exercise and leafy green diet, Earl's body was tight and his eyes were clear. Even his speech was coherent, from hours of work rehearsing his talking points.

Earl had evolved into the very essence of a Republican presidential candidate.

'My fellow Americans! And I mean you! The real Americans! Not those fancy-pants democrats with their so-called education and communism!'

The crowd responded instantly. This was what they came to hear.

'I am here for the honest, hard-working Americans! Americans who believe in God and his son Jesus Christ!'

The crowd went wild.

"I owns twenty guns! You know why? Because guns is freedom! Good Christian Americans loves theys freedom! You know what else I love? I love coal! I sleep on a bed of coal! I eat coal for breakfast! You know why? Because I am a real American and coal is good for America!"

'Too much with the coal?' Kenny asked Alicia.

Alicia watched the crowd as they chanted, 'Earl! Earl! Earl!'

'Er, no. I think you nailed the coal,' Alicia told him. To her surprise she was getting a serious chub for Kenny. Kenny sensed her chub and took a step back.

'When I gets sick, I don't wants the government to pay for my doctor. That's communism! Real Americans hate communists! Free medicine is communism! Are y'all real Americans? Do y'all hate communists?'

'Real Americans!' the crowd chanted.

At that moment "EARL FOR PRESIDENT" banners started appearing, and everybody wanted one.

Thousands of banners were being waved about hysterically. Then right on cue, huge bags of "EARL" balloons opened-up and dropped from the ceiling, while fireworks exploded from the stage.

'Earl! Earl! Earl!' the crowd screamed, going completely wild.

Thousands of in-bred hillbillies came together as one. They had their man, the man who represented them.

In the final days of the convention the votes were tallied, and Earl won the nomination by a massive majority in an almost unprecedented floor vote. All the hard-earned state candidate primary votes were cast aside.

The other top-ranked GOP hopefuls were stunned beyond belief. They had endured a year of pre-selection campaigning, fundraising and debates. Yet Earl skipped right past all that. Frankly, they were dull and boring next to the amazing Earl.

Kenny and his team knew Republican voters don't like facts, policy agendas, or word structures that require thought. They just wanted a simpleton. A simpleton just like them. They wanted Earl.

'We need to abduct more Fox News people,' Kenny told Alicia.

She nodded and smiled at Kenny, using her teeth and mouth.

What the fuck is happening? Kenny asked himself. *Does Alicia actually have a chub for me?*

Alicia read his mind and nodded. Kenny became very scared.

Over the next two nights the Seabertian abduction and data transfer teams were busier than a one-hoofed Trigoatigan in a three-legged hover-hoop race.

They abducted a plethora of Fox News on and off camera staff, including presenters, producers and a few sixth-floor senior managers.

Kenny's strategy was to burst the GOP bubble at the perfect moment. He knew the average voter had the memory span of a West Zillian gnat, the mythical bug that only lived for four minutes.

He would wait for the perfect moment, then obliterate their hand-made presidential candidate, and the entire GOP apparatus.

When Todd Splick discovered this, he furiously dialled up Admiral Gustov.

'You've got to call off your people, Admiral,' Splick said.

'Oh, yes?' the admiral replied.

'If the Americans elect Earl, *Reality Earth* TV will rate through the roof for four more years.' Splick was speaking very loudly.

'Splick! You are not talking to one of your olikian coffee blow-job boys. Quiet the fuck down!'

'Sorry, sir. It's just that if your people kill Earl off in the campaign, we will be left with nothing. The Democratic candidate is a very reasonable person. The chance of either a major fuck-up or scandal are very slim.'

'So?' The admiral knew exactly what Splick wanted, but was going to make him say it.

'Admiral, you retire in six months. I am in position to make you a very rich man. I'll give you a lucrative contract with our broadcasting network,' Splick told him.

'If I play ball and let Earl become president? Thus, ruining any chance of Earth joining the Dignified League of Galactic Worlds?' the admiral asked.

'Correct! There is nothing more important than the ratings,' Splick pushed.

'I don't give a toss-fried Degarian egg about your fucking ratings. However, I have recorded this call and your attempted extortion.'

The admiral leaned back in his very large chair and started playing with his dick.

Todd Splick said something uncivilised in Welsh and hung up.

***

The Earl for President campaign was gaining momentum across the heartland of America. Polls had them winning everywhere, including in many swing states.

'If this momentum continues, he'll get some three hundred and twenty electoral votes,' Alicia reported.

Kenny smiled as he watched his creation finishing his fourth stump speech for the day at a lumber yard in South Carolina. Kenny marvelled at how Earl's simplistic nonsense rallied the people.

'I will bring back American manufacturing,' Earl told them loudly. 'More jobs mean better wages for you! More cars, better holidays, better everything! For you! The real Americans!'

The cheers went up, and the music started.

'How many more of these do we have to endure?' Alicia asked.

'About one hundred,' Kenny told her.

'Can we do that thing again tonight?' she asked.

'That thing where you wrap your legs around my head—' Kenny was rudely interrupted by Karen Jacobs from CNN.

'Kenny Kendrick! You're a hard man to get hold of!' Karen told him.

Alicia stared at Karen and she took a step back.

'You only get to speak to Kenny through me,' Alicia told her.

Karen's sphincter tightened.

'All I want is an interview with candidate Earl,' Karen told her.

'Earl doesn't have time to give interviews to CNN,' Alicia told her.

'How is that democracy? If your candidate won't speak to half the country?' Karen complained.

'Your version of democracy is biased, and besides, we don't like you.' Alicia stood with hands on hips.

Karen smiled like a viper and marched away.

Earl raced up to them. 'How'd I do, boss?'

'Wonderful, Earl! You're a champion of the people!' Kenny patted him on the back. 'A genuine Republican president.'

Alicia wanted to throw up in her mouth but formed a big smiley face for Earl.

Earl blushed at her in return.

'Let's go find a gym!' Earl told them. 'Then I'll need my protein shake.'

He marched off toward the campaign bus.

'We may have gone a little heavy with the gym thing,' Kenny told Alicia.

'Mmm,' Alicia said absently. She was busy planning a menu of ways she'd allow Kenny to please her that night.

The Zeet Crisis

Every galaxy in the universe has at least one completely messed-up species of beings, and the Milky Way Galaxy has the Zeet.

If you asked anyone on Earth to draw a picture of an alien, they would draw a Zeet. There's a very good reason for that.

The Zeet have been abducting Earthlings for an eon. They arrive in the dark, float into people's homes, and scare the living daylights out them. Not to mention the free space rides, painful medical experiments and anal probing.

To the casual observer, it seems the Zeet just can't get enough Earthling ass.

But why are the Zeet so nasty? One theory, supported by many in the galaxy, describes the Zeet as suffering from small alien syndrome. For as we know, size, particularly in the Milky Way Galaxy, is very important.

Inter-galactic travellers report this problem does not exist in other galaxies. Andromeda, for example, like their aliens to be smaller. They enjoy a more comfortable, easy fit , rather than brute size and watering eyes.

The Zeet are also the physical antitheses of humanoid species like Earthlings and Seabertians.

Typically, they are four-feet tall, with grey clammy skin and over-sized heads. Compounding this, their spindly bodies do nothing to enhance their already piss poor appearance.

This in-your-face physical disparity causes the Zeet to hate all the "pretty" humanoid galactic beings with every pore of their grey tacky skin.

Galactic debate still rages over whether it's the fact they are grey, short and spindly that makes them nasty or they're just nasty regardless. Many a galactic scholar will shrug, scratch his head, then change the subject to football.

Here's the rub; Earth was not a member of the Dignified League of Galactic Planets. As such, Zillian Zeet, the Zeet king and sole unelected leader of the Zeet world, knew Earthlings had no legal protection.

By definition, planet Earth, and all who lived there, were wide open to all levels of exploitation. Except for the excellent blooper-reel entertainment Earthlings provide, no one in the galaxy gave a toss about their well-being.

As a result of this vulnerability, Zillian Zeet abducted Earthlings for specific elements of their DNA and stole bits from Earthling livestock.

From the harvested Earthling DNA, the Zeet "grew" huge free-labour workforces to do all the shitty jobs in the Zeetian Empire. Theses miserable jobs included new planet terra-forming, sanitation, food production, retail and hospitality.

Due to an inherent Zeetian-level lack of imagination, millions of these clones were named David or Terrance.

However, when working in groups, it was often necessary to create variations of these names to avoid confusion.

The snotty clones called themselves David. The cute ones became Davey. Dumb ones were Davo. The groovy ones became Dave. Crazy ones were labelled Wee Mental Davey. Fat ones became Big-D. Gay ones, Love-Me-Some-D. Horny ones, Got-You-Some-Fat D.

It must be said that this last group of Daves were rare and spent a lot of time alone.

Along the Terrance name-line, similar themes were applied.

Why only males, some ask? Why not clone female DNA as well and make breeding pairs? The reason is a simple legal technicality.

If a labour force is solely produced from cloned cells, that clone exists outside the galactic laws of slavery. Clones are classified as "property" of the clone manufacturer.

If females were present, and they mated with the cloned males, the offspring would legally fail the clone test and this would ruin the entire programme.

Bottom line: in the Zeet clone enterprise, it was a strictly no chicks allowed scenario.

As you can imagine, the clone slave labour trade evolved into a huge downstream profit-centre for Zeetian industry.

They were able to clone Earthlings for their labour exchanges, and breed a new variant of galactic cattle which was very popular when lightly seared and served medium rare.

However, being witless anti-humourists, the Zeet never watched the *Reality Earth* TV channel. As such, it took them weeks to learn the smartass Seabertians were working hard to help Earth evolve and become dignified.

Eventually, the Seabertian plan was brought to the attention of the king.

'If Earth is awarded a dignified status, how much will it cost us?' Zillian Zeet asked his finance minister, a man called Izt.

'Four xtrons each month, Sire,' Izt told his king. 'The clone programme and the livestock harvesting will both become outlawed. I'm not sure what the galactic counsel will order regarding all the David and Terrance clones. There's a chance we'll have to set them free. I'm not sure where we can re-house ten million clones who are only qualified to use shovels. North Dakota, I suppose.'

'Four xtrons a month! Fuck my zore!' Zillian Zeet screamed.

It must be explained that a Seabertian or Earthling scream sounds completely unlike a Zeetian scream. A Zeet scream sounds a lot more like a small tree monkey with his penis caught in a cluster of zillberry thorns.

'Sire, it will mean the decommissioning of five-star cruisers, and retiring half our army,' Izt announced, readying himself for a slap.

Zillian Zeet did indeed slap him. But being slapped by a Zeet felt more like being hit with a moist towelette.

'Very good, Sire,' Izt thanked him.

'Now fuck off and summon my generals!' Zillian Zeet commanded.

The Zeet, even the big ones, only weighed thirty pounds. In their low gravity, misty world, they tended to hop-drift along the ground, a bit like bunny ghost rabbits.

King Zillian-Zeet sat on his throne and watched his generals hop-drift into the royal audience chamber. Zillian was fond of all things French and designed all of his fifty palaces along eighteenth-century architectural lines. The tapestries, chandeliers and stained-glass windows all gave the impression of someone trying too hard to be French, but not actually getting there.

Galactic dignitaries who visited Zeetland often came away with the feeling they needed a bath. They said it was like being trapped inside a French brothel.

Zillian's mood was now one of pure loathing, as each of his generals performed their elaborate Zeetian salute by waving their arms about and offering a floppy bow.

When this process finally ended , they seated themselves on the audience bench before their king.

Zillian thought his generals were inbred halfwits, and the ones who weren't he suspected of future sedition. Despite this, he could not fire them as they were all related, in one way or another, to his precious wife.

She was one hundred years younger than him and gave the best noodle-pull in three worlds. 'No wife's generals, no noodle-pull,' she often reminded him.

'I hope that by now you have all been briefed on the latest bullshit the Seabertians are trying to pull on Earth?' Zillian asked them.

The generals nodded, all except one.

'I haven't,' Calamitous-Zeet declared. In Zeetland, there is always one.

'Then fuck off and ask someone!' King Zillian yelled, or squeaked, depending on your galactic understanding of yelling.

Calamitous jumped up and pushed off the bench a little too hard, hitting his head on the ceiling. He squeaked in pain, then hop-floated off toward the door.

'The Seabertian scum are trying to screw us one more time! And frankly, I've had enough of their bullshit to last me four lifetimes,' Zillian began. 'The Earthling slave DNA and cattle trades are vital to my military industry. That means you bunch of inbred Greamling-fuckers!'

The generals absorbed the insult with practised apathy. However, their king did speak the truth. The generals loved a roll in the dry legas with a horny Greamling, and they were all the offspring of brother-sister marriages.

'I want you to send a fully armed cruiser to Earth and scare the shit out of their man there, a Seabertian named Kenny Kendrick,' King Zillian ordered.

The generals knew this order violated at least seven galactic council laws. They also knew that if they complained, Zillian-Zeet would violate them in the most unholy fashion.

'You are to find Kendrick and abduct him. Then conduct a full explorative procedure on him,' Zillian-Zeet commanded.

The generals blanched again. They had never probed a member of an inducted civilisation before. It was a direct violation of the peace accord and resulted in the death of the assailant.

Zillian-Zeet could sense their hesitation.

'If anyone finds out, you can say you made a mistake. Say you didn't know Kenny was a Seabertian, blah blah,' Zillian-Zeet told them reassuringly. 'Don't worry, I'll have your backs.'

The generals knew all about Zillian-Zeet having their backs. Five hundred years hence, Zillian killed his parents to become king and get a free ticket to the orphans' picnic.

'I think this vital mission will go to you, General Jleek,' Zillian-Zeet announced.

Jleek died a little death, but as the Zeet have no facial features, Jleek could only blink his huge eyes.

'Thank you, Sire,' Jleek told his king and bowed deeply, banging his head on his knees. *I'd love to perform an exploration on you*, he thought.

The Republican Demolition Derby
Ten days out from the Presidential election

Alicia was feeling well satisfied having completed a two-hour session using Kenny's face for her sexual relief. Then, after much begging, she allowed Kenny a full thirty seconds to use her body for his pleasure.

'You want me for thirty seconds!' Alicia cried. 'Holy Gods, Kenny! It'll feel like forever!'

As Kenny rushed to finish, he knew Alicia was a real deJong. Yet, he loved her anyway.

They showered separately, as Alicia hated being touched after sex. She liked to separate sex with Kenny from her emotional state. Having no actual love-based emotions, this was easy for her.

They dressed separately and joined the campaign team for a breakfast meeting.

Kenny, despite being sexually abused by Alicia for half the night, was in a very positive mood. All his plans for helping the Earthlings would come to pass this very night.

'Today is the day!' Kenny opened the team meeting. 'Rebekah and Amanda will be babysitting Earl through five stump speeches in five states. You guys need to do this without speaking to anyone from CNN.'

The two ensigns moaned. They were getting sick and tired of this election bullshit that seemed to go on forever. State after state, the same boring stump speech infinitum.

'Then you must get Earl back to the Fox News studios in Denver, Colorado by eight p.m.,' Kenny said firmly. 'No matter what it takes. He must be back here by eight.'

'What are you three doing?' Amanda asked.

'We've got a busy day of none of your fucking business!' Alicia snapped at her. 'Now, go get Earl out of the gym and hit the road.'

Amanda sighed again at the thought of enduring another long day with Earl, who was always wanting a gym session or a protein shake. But she knew better than to complain as Alicia looked a bit slap happy.

'All righty then,' Kenny said, full of enthusiasm. 'Today's the day we destroy the US Republican Party and Fox News all in one huge hit. Today we save planet Earth!'

Alicia offered a lacklustre smile. She couldn't give a flying toss about saving Earth any more. She just wanted her new assignment in a way cooler part of the galaxy.

'As you know, when we abducted the Fox News people, they were given an activation code to trigger their new personalities,' Kenny remined them. 'Right now, they are the same hypocrites, liars and fearmongers they have always been. But tonight, a bomb goes off! Tonight, the Earth changes forever!'

Kenny picked up his cell phone and dialled a number.

'Hi, Lucy?' Kenny asked. 'It's Kenny from the campaign. Oh, and you too. Take a picture of my what? No, I can't do that, I'm with people. Meet later? I'd love to but my face is sore and... oh, no, nothing like that. I, ah, just had it squashed under... it doesn't matter. What I'm calling for is, Earl wants to come on the Garety show. Tonight, would be great! Oh yeah, Earl is the man! I've got to run, bye!'

He hung up and stared at his phone for a second, then looked up to see Alicia glaring at him.

'What?' he asked her.

Kenny turned to Kyle who had a stupid grin on his face.

'Try to forget everything you just heard,' Kenny told him. 'I have a special assignment for you.'

Kyle moaned. He hated Kenny's special assignments.

'I need you to write a Twitter post and send it to everyone,' Kenny told him. 'The message is: "Don't miss tonight's Earl interview on Fox with Garety. Something big will be revealed."'

Later that day...

The Zeet star cruiser approached Earth from behind the moon, manoeuvring toward a geostationary orbit position on the far side.

'Send out the probes,' General Jleek told his first officer. 'Be extra stealthy now, I don't want the *Mercurial-Blue* alerted.'

'Extra stealthy! Yes, sir!' the first officer repeated.

Four probes left the cruiser heading toward the Earth. An hour passed until the first report came in.

'Sir! We have found the Seabertians!' The first officer activated his brand-new 3D holographic display device that showed Earth and the Seabertian ship.

'Nice hologram, Number One,' Jleek said, causing the younger Zeet to blink with pride.

Number One loved his General. Not in a Todd Splick-Geon Plume, sweaty male on male way. More like when a boy has a favourite uncle who doesn't want to wrestle all the time.

As the Zeet cruiser circled quietly around the Earth, it managed to avoid detection by the *Mercurial Blue*. The Zeet probes entered the Earth's atmosphere, commencing their search for Kenny Kendrick.

It took a while for the drones to acquire them, as Kenny and Alicia were in a commercial jet flying to Denver, Colorado, the city where Earl was to do his Garety interview.

The probes were programmed to track Kenny's eye and audio transmission signal frequency which the Zeet crew had hacked from the network.

The first probe found Kenny's jet and wheeled around behind it, settling in behind and below the jet's tail. It then followed Kenny all the way into Denver.

Still tuned into Kenny's communication frequency, Jleek and Number One were forced to endure Kenny's conversation with Alicia.

'So, do you love her?' Alicia asked.

'Who?' Kenny was getting nervous.

'Garety's fox news producer,' Alicia said, as a sharp tone entered her voice.

'Her? Are you kidding?' Kenny asked.

'Why did she want a picture of your dick then?' Alicia drilled in.

'Maybe she simply likes photography. Did you think of that?' He knew that was pretty lame, but it was all he could think of.

Alicia grabbed Kenny's phone, shoved it down her pants and took a picture.

'What the fuck are you doing!' Kenny yelled.

Alicia scrolled through his contact list and found the producer. Before Kenny could stop her, she sent the poor girl the image.

'I hope she likes my photography too,' Alicia told him and handed back the phone.

'Did that just happen?' Jleek asked Number One.

'From what I know about the Seabertians, sir, it most certainly did.'

'Did we also intercept the image?' Jleek asked.

'I can check, sir,' Number One told his boss.

'You might need to do that, Number One. You know, for the mission log.'

As Kenny's plane landed, the trailingZeet drone climbed high in the sky and remained out of sight.

Within minutes, all four drones had descended on the city, commencing their surveillance.

'This will be a tough one, sir,' Number One told his general. 'Kendrick is in a hotel room, in the centre of the city.'

'We have no choice. We shall grab him in his hotel room,' the general said, feeling quite ill with the knowledge he was about to violate a sacred galactic law.

'He is not alone, sir,' Number One advised. 'What shall we do with the others?'

'Well fuck my goat, Number One! We'll just have to grab them too!' the general swore, in a rare display of irritation.

Abducting one Seabertian was bad. Grabbing a room full of the genetically modified cock-wallys was a political nightmare.

'This needs to go perfectly, Number One, or we'll all burn,' the general said quietly, regaining his composure.

'Yes, sir.' Number One shared the general's tension and was feeling quite nervous. So nervous, in fact, he needed to do a number two.

The Zeet abduction team spent the remainder of their time rehearsing a hotel room abduction. When satisfied, they boarded their transport and flew toward Denver.

'We're all set, sir,' Number One told General Jleek. 'We have Kendrick's position on the twentieth floor and the abduction team is on the roof.'

'Execute!' The general gave the order.

Kenny, Alicia and Kyle were fixated on their hotel TV. The Garety show was about to start and Earl was in the studio, being fluffed by Amanda and Rebecca.

Kenny began to twitch. This was the moment he had dreamed about for two years since being assigned to observe Earth.

'Who wants a drink?' he asked his team.

'Shit yes!' both Alicia and Kyle said in unison.

'Let's not do that again,' Alicia told Kyle.

They all placed orders, and Kyle went for the fluffy duck. He had a strange yet undefinable love for fluffy cocktails.

A loud knock came at the door.

'That was fast,' Kyle said, and jumped up to answer it.

As he opened the door the Zeet abduction team leader flashed him with a stun gun, and he went down. Before Kenny could react, the Zeet were in the room and stunned him too.

Alicia was much faster than the boys, and jumped to her feet. She launched herself at the attackers but was hit mid-stride before she could reach them. She arched her back and fell face down on the carpet with her arse stuck up into the air.

The Zeet team stood and stared.

'That's some pretty sweet arse, boys,' one said.

'Squeak-squeak,' his teammates agreed.

The Zeets placed the paralysed Seabertians in bags and dumped them onto hover trollies.

'Big bastards,' one of the Zeets complained.

'Squeak,' another replied.

On their way back to the ship, the Zeet encountered a few more Earthlings who got a good stunning for their troubles.

They reached the roof and loaded the Seabertians onboard. After a brief climb, and a flash of bright light, the transport was gone.

'Don't forget to wash your hands, guys. You don't know where these Seabertians have been,' the abduction team leader told his people. A round of squeaks in agreement followed.

Fifteen minutes later, the prone Seabertians were coming around. One by one they opened their eyes to see a Zeet staring down at them.

'Are you fucking idiots serious?' Alicia yelled. 'Have you actually abducted us?'

'Shut the fuck up, Alicia,' the Zeet told her.

How does he know my name, she wondered. *Must be by reputation*, she guessed.

As it happened, Alicia had never slept with a Zeet. They were one of the very few galactic species she hadn't knocked over to this point.

It took a minute for Kenny to catch up with live events. He was always a little slow witted after a good plastering.

'Oh, suck my greasy ort! You grey Greamling-fuckers are all dead! Galactic law 782-920-TS clearly states—' Kenny began.

'*Shut up*, Kenny!' General Jleet squeaked. 'We know all about your stupid plan to make Earth nice by eliminating all things Republican. But let me tell you this! We Zeets will lose a huge amount of ching-ching if that happens.'

'You money grubbing pack of arseholes!' Kenny was now fully pissed off. 'This mission was approved by Galactic Star Corp. Send us back right now, or they'll have your nuts.'

Kenny had a doubt. 'Do you guys actually have nuts?'

'We have noodles! *Noodles*!' the Zeet squeaked at him. 'Let your Earthling Earl win this election and put the Republicans in power, then we'll let you go. Easy peezy, nothing sleazy.' The general had recently heard that saying on *Reality Earth* TV and really liked it.

'Too late, Zeet!' Kenny told him. 'The whole filthy Republican house of cards is about to crumble. Do you have cable TV on this piece of shit?'

The general made a motion toward his first officer, who promptly switched on the big TV.

'Tune it to Fox,' Kenny told him.

As they watched, the Garety show had already started. Josh Garety was busy humping Earl's leg over his love for guns, coal and Jesus. Earl was seconds away from speaking the magic words to activate Garety's new brain-transfer data.

Right there, on the big TV in the Zeet ship, and in millions of homes throughout the southern and midwestern United States, the pivotal moment struck.

'You know, Josh, I really love Christmas,' Earl told Garety. 'I love Santa Claus, Christmas carols and guns. In fact, my favourite saying is, deck the halls with guns and ammo!'

Garety's head twitched as though he'd been slapped. In a micro-second, his very small brain re-booted with its new data programme.

Josh Garety switched from being a fully corrupt right-wing stooge to a human being. He took a moment to look around him, and it began.

'There were over seven hundred mass shootings across America last year, Earl,' Josh Garety began. 'How do you think all the real American mothers, fathers, brothers and sisters of these victims feel right now, when you say, "Deck the halls with guns and ammo"?'

It took a few seconds for Earl to process the question.

When he finally understood it, Earl looked like he'd been punched in the gut. He had no idea what to say. He was not trained to answer this question and all cognition abandoned him.

'Okay, let's make it simple for you.' Garety started a new thought. 'Do you think it's normal that children going to school should be shot to death by sociopaths with easy access to military assault weapons?'

Earl recovered somewhat and fell back on his talking points.

'What about freedom, Josh?' Earl asked. ' 'Owning lots of guns means freedom!'

'How is owning guns that are only designed to kill people freedom, Earl?' Garety asked. 'Besides that, I register my car and my boat. I register my dog. I need a building permit to put up a garden shed. I even need a licence to catch a fish. I can also lose my driver's licence if I develop a serious mental condition. Yet, I can keep my guns. Does that sound cool and normal to you?'

'It's all a slippery slope, Josh,' Earl said weakly, feeling the ground crumble under his feet.

'Tell me this, Earl. You want freedom? Freedom from laws? Freedom from safety?' Garety honed in. ' As the GOP presidential candidate, will you abolish driver's licence tests? Will you abolish building permits? After all, these take away my freedom to drive dangerously and erect unstable buildings.'

Josh Garety was speaking slowly and clearly, waiting patiently for Earl's reply.

'It's all about freedom!' Earl was yelling now. 'Americans needs theys freedom!'

Earl was sweating and started flapping his arms like a pregnant duck.

'Do dead massacred children and their families have freedom, Earl?' Garety asked.

'They are collateral damage, Josh. They suffer so that we can have our freedom! It's all about freedom!' Earl had completely unspooled. He looked directly into the camera with the little red light and started yelling. 'USA! USA! USA! Murika! Murika! Murika!'

To the relief of everyone watching, the producer cut Earl's mic feed and put the cameras back on Garety.

'Ladies and gentlemen,' Garety started wrapping up, 'this is Earl, and he wants to be your president. A few months ago, he was a meth-head and an alcoholic. He lived in a piss-filled shipping container with his dogs. Like all Republican politicians, he has no social policies and his only agenda is to give tax breaks to billionaires. Good luck, folks. I hope you live through his presidency!'

General Jleet smacked his forehead with his flimsy baby-hand. He had failed in his mission and knew he was done.

'Phaser the Seabertians and take them back to the hotel,' he told Number One.

'Hey! You don't have to phaser...' Kenny did not get to complete his plea, as 50,000 volts hit his brain.

In the Fox News office people ran up and down the corridors waving their arms and screaming. The phrase "What the fuck!" was yelled one thousand six hundred and forty-two times.

Damage control teams were assembled and a counter-story was under construction. It went along the lines of: "Josh Garety had a mental breakdown after a long battle with drugs, alcohol and an addiction to transgender prostitution."

In studio-eight, the Fox cameras switched to Mandy Keeler. She was known as the "bride of Satan" to everyone in the USA who had more than five minutes of high school.

Fox management knew she'd save the day.

Yet, seconds before she went live, her phone rang. It was her mother's emergency number. When she hit the answer key a voice said, 'HiMandy, deck the halls with guns and ammo.'

Mandy's head twitched and she started speaking to camera.

Fifteen seconds later, the programme director cut her feed, running their code-red standby tape on American Heroes.

In the following days, a pandemic of reality broke out in the right-wing media. Every corrupt media presenter on the right had changed their message to reality and common sense.

The American airwaves were free from hate-based propaganda for the first time in three decades. It was replaced with messages denouncing gun violence, climate change, corporate tax avoidance and Pentagon corruption.

Even the new breed of young wannabe right-wing presenters called out the crazies, and without Fox propaganda, Earl's numbers plummeted faster than a lead bitcoin.

GOP candidates running in house and senate races also trailed by double digit points, as the American heartland was placed on a diet of reason and logic.

Even the most ardent hard-core, trailer-trash, illiterate hillbillies were developing serious doubts.

Thousands of southern state bars and trailer parks that normally ran Fox News twenty-four-seven unplugged their TVs.

GOP leadership was being hammered from all sides. Lobbyists from all the trillion-dollar empires, including; energy, fire arms, fast food, health, pharmaceutical, chemical, agriculture, petrochemical, and the heaviest hitters of them all, the American weapons industry, screamed blue murder as their right-wing media propaganda machines broke down.

The corporations that had made Americans sick and stolen their money for generations depended on the Republican Party for their very survival. Now they were exposed like cockroaches in the bright kitchen light.

On the fortieth floor of the New York Smeiser building, a group of old men sat around a large, heavy timber ornate table.

The meeting was called by the American Weapons Manufacturers' Association. They were some of the richest people on Earth, yet unlike the new breed of blue-flame, hot-shot billionaires, they were old-money men and remained invisible to the general population.

In fact, they paid vast sums of cash each year to their PR firms to remain so. Just like the invisible mafia; if you were noticed by the media, you got a bullet to the head. Figuratively speaking, of course.

On the other side of the table were the owners of right-wing media companies. These men were about to get reamed like a 1970s' Rectorian porn star attempting an inter-galactic gang-bang record.

Double-backed burgundy drapes covered the windows from floor to ceiling, these old men hated natural light as it burned their skin. They preferred the soft hued, indirect lighting that gave the room a more fitting dystopian feel.

Large men with earpieces and loopy wires that disappeared under their suits stood guard in the hallways outside the conference room doors.

It made the old men feel secure to have armed guards close by.

***

Over one trillion homes throughout the galaxy had now tuned into *Reality Earth Live* TV show. The show had already received nominations for best comedy; now it was under serious consideration for best drama.

Todd Splick and Geon Plume were completely captivated by their own creation. Ching, ching, ching, flowed the cash.

***

Back in the Smeiser building boardroom, the reaming was about to begin.

'We paid you scumbags over one fifty billion dollars last year to do one simple, straightforward job.' Leo Spleetz, chairman of Wright Aviation opened the meeting. 'Keep everyone below the Mason-Dixon and in the Midwest ignorant and blind to our activities. To stand in the rain with their mouths open like the fucking turkey that drowns itself.'

Leo Spleetz stared at the media men with cold dead eyes. If this was Russia, he told himself, he could have all these men thrown out the window. Bad fucking luck this was America, he fumed.

He held up his hand and a man came forth with a huge cigar. The man lit the cigar as Spleetz rolled it and puffed, filling the room with blue smoke.

He waited until someone coughed.

'Your one job was to keep an inherently ignorant poplution confused and angry, so that they never look at us. Sex scandals, conspiracies, lies and fearmongering on one continuous loop. That's all we asked of you.'

The media bosses lowered their heads and stared at the table. They had failed their lord and master.

'What the hell happened out there?' Spleetz asked. 'How did dozens of over-paid media personalities all switch sides at the same time?'

'We've had psychiatrists and psychologists examine our presenters,' Desmond Grimes, the right-wing media spokesperson told Spleetz. 'Their findings were inconclusive. Every one of them had a different theory on how a person can achieve an almost instant mind shift in their core beliefs and act out against their best interests.'

There was a long pause.

'We know how it happened.' Another man spoke up. He was a younger man, with a Sharp andDangerous look about him. 'They were hypnotised.'

'Oh, come on! How can you possibly know that!' Des Grimes asked before he could stop himself.

'Really, Mister Grimes?' Sharp-and-Dangerous asked in a voice that made small children cry. 'You are talking to the heart of America's defence industry here. When we speak, you listen.'

This was the first time in forty years Des Grimes didn't know what to say. So he put his face on screen-saver mode.

'Not only do we build weapons that can vaporise cities, but we also work with the CIA on more exotic applications; including brain-washing,' Sharp-and-Dangerous told him. 'How do you think we get so many ex-beauty queens and self-declared Christian men to line up and sell their souls to the devil, working for right wing media organisations?'

Grimes asked himself that question all the time. He assumed it was the money.

'You see, Grimes, we are all under attack,' Leo Spleetz announced. 'If we don't find out who's doing this and stop them, two things will happen. The GOP will be out of power across the board in the United States, and we will be shut down.'

Spleetz drew a long puff on his cigar, letting the ash tumble off onto the table. Everyone followed its fall until it disintegrated on the hard surface.

'The F-35 stealth fighter contract earned us one-point-five trillion dollars and the costs are still climbing,' Sharp-and-Dangerous began. 'The joke is, we already had a fifth-generation stealth fighter in the F-22. We are building new aircraft carriers, and replacing entire fleets of helicopters, tanks and missiles. Trillions of dollars' worth of weapons that will never see a war, and all this expenditure is in peacetime. So, how do we get away with it?'

They all knew the answer, but Des Grimes said it anyway. 'Because the GOP and its right-wing media propaganda machine spins fearmongering twenty-four hours a day, seven days a week, to the paranoid, uneducated white masses. Yes, I think we all know that. And just who are you anyway?' Grimes asked Sharp-and-Dangerous.

Sharp-and-Dangerous stared back at him. 'I'm the last person you will see before the lights go out.'

Grimes viewed Sharp-and-Dangerous. He knew at once this guy was not fucking around.

Grimes shifted his attention back to Leo Spleetz.

'What will you have us do?' Des Grimes asked his lord.

'Hit social media with everything you have,' Spleetz told him. 'The CIA will send you files of material to smash the Democrats. We predict whoever is behind this will have the technology to stop you, and that will tip their hand.'

'A trap?' Grimes asked.

Spleetz smiled and blew a massive stream of smoke up to the ceiling. Everyone coughed and wiped tears from their eyes.

***

After two days of near-empty stump speech venues, Team Kenny took Earl back to the campaign war-room at the GOP head office in Washington, DC.

The GOP leadership resembled a bunch of children who'd had their Disney Plus subscription cancelled. The election was just a few days out, and they had no hope of victory.

That night in the campaign hotel suite, Team Kenny ordered room service and margaritas.

'Fox has gone on a social media blitz,' Kyle told them. 'Look at some of the shit they've posted.'

'Makes sense. It's the only media outlet they have left,' Alicia said. 'Do we hit back?'

'We've gone this far,' Kenny said. 'May as well go all the way.'

Alicia smiled. She got a fast chub for Kenny. Kenny sensed the chub and flinched.

Kenny touched his ear. 'James! Still awake?'

James had been camped out in the *Mercurial Blue* DIC for weeks now. He was tired, lonely, and more than a little shitty.

'Of course I'm fucking here! I never leave here! I really hate here!' James told them, in state of near unspooling.

'Hang in there, pal,' Kenny tried to soothe him. 'This will be over soon.'

'Yeah, right, Kenny. What do you want?'

'I need you to hack all the social media accounts from the right and give them a dirty big virus. In fact, hack their credit accounts and divert all their money to the Save the Children of Mexico charity. Then place them on a permanent rotating block list. Oh, and just for fun, change all their passwords and lock them out entirely.'

'I can do that,' James told him, sounding a little more cheerful.

'Use our Chinese and Russian servers, I don't want any fingerprints on this,' Kenny advised him.

James smiled. He liked hacking almost as much as he liked watching Kenny's bedtime eye camera feeds.

***

The next day, Leo Spleetz met privately with Sharp-and-Dangerous.

'Where did the hacks originate?' Spleetz asked.

'The usual suspects,' Sharp-and-Dangerous told him. 'But that means nothing. My sources in Russia and China tell me they themselves were hijacked by a third party. They used a code no one has seen before, and the speed of the hack was a thousand times faster than anything used before.'

'So what the fuck does that mean?' Spleetz was becoming nervous. 'Our people were supposed to be all powerful, now there's a new player?'

'I have a theory,' Sharp-and-Dangerous began. 'But you won't like it.'

'Try me,' Spleetz told him.

'Who has the power to brainwash, en masse, in complete secrecy, if not us?' Sharp-and-Dangerous asked rhetorically. 'Who else has the power to hijack the entire internet in one day?'

Leo Spleetz reached for a cigar. 'You've got to be fucking kidding me,' he finally said.

'There's been a significant uplift in UFO activity lately,' Sharp-and-Dangerous said. 'Our people in the air force have been tracking all sorts of craft flying in and out of our airspace over the past few weeks.'

Spleetz was quiet for a long time.

'Do you think they're making a move?' he asked Sharp-and-Dangerous.

'If they are, it's long overdue. Getting rid of the GOP will help clean up the mess down here. It's a great first step.'

'Disaster and opportunity are two sides of the same coin,' Spleetz announced. 'I want you to war game this out. Get your people assembled and come up with a plan. If these aliens are getting ready to pop the hatch and say hi, I want to lead the process.'

Sharp-and-Dangerous smiled for his master. 'One more thing,' Sharpe-and-Dangerous began. 'The so- called political operative, Kenny Kendrick. Many in the GOP have no idea who he is. The strategy team hired him, but they can't remember why.'

'Oh, yes?' Spleetz said. The hairs on the back of his neck were rising.

'I'm pretty sure he's one of them. Here's a picture of Kendrick and his team.' Sharp-and-Dangerous swiped his phone and gave it to Spleetz.

Spleetz stared at the five tall, impossibly beautiful young people.

'Where are you going to find five political consultants, all working together in the one team, that look like that?' Sharp-and-Dangerous asked his master.

'Why in the name of God's crotch didn't this come up earlier?' Spleetz asked.

'They were winning, sir. Earl was hands-down in front,' Sharp-and-Dangerous told him. 'Do you want us to grab Kendrick?'

Leo Spleetz took a long pull on his cigar.

'Are you asking me if I want to "grab" an alien?' Spleetz asked with cold dead eyes. 'While they are planning first contact? Thereby fucking our chances of being the moderators in the big show?'

Sharp-and-Dangerous froze his face.

Spleetz decided to let his young protege off the hook and laughed.

'I agree, it would be fun.' Spleetz grinned. 'But no, I have another idea. We need to do something bold.'

'How bold, sir? Domestic or international?' Sharp-and-Dangerous asked.

'International,' Spleetz told him.

Sharp-and-Dangerous knew what "bold" and "international" meant. He viewed his master with great reverence. This was why Leo Spleetz was the one true master of America, and Dark Lord of the Industrial Military Complex.

***

The election was held with the lowest turnout in US voting history. The result was called that night by ten p.m. on the West Coast, and the Democratic Party won everything up and down the ticket in a 75% landslide.

Team Kenny watched Earl stumble through his concession speech in the Washington hotel ballroom. His brain transfer was wearing off and he had stopped going to the gym and showering. He had also returned to his hot dog diet.

Kenny judged him ready for his return to the Kentucky dog piss office.

'Our work here is done, people,' Kenny told his team. 'Time to head home.'

'Can't we stay a little longer? I have some shopping to do and we still have lots of money,' Rebekah asked. She had turned native, Kenny saw. Her world had become all about the bling.

'The colonel has ordered us back, but I could really use a drink,' Alicia announced. 'Earth is fun, if you're young, rich and pretty.'

'Okay then, one more night,' Kenny conceded. 'Kyle! Find us a nightclub.'

The Impending War
The Pentagon, Washington DC

The very moment the GOP lost its footing in American politics, the joint chiefs called a meeting in the secure briefing room on sub-level five. These men were all tied to the Military Industrial Complex (MIC), right down to their DNA.

Leon Spleetz, Sharp-and-Dangerous, and all the major weapons' manufacturing CEOs were in attendance.

The chiefs may have started their careers as honest soldiers, airmen and sailors, but now they were old white men who knew what money was used for. They all owned multiple large homes, drove very expensive cars, and kept ex-model mistresses.

The chiefs viewed their MIC lords and masters.

These men had the power to provide an excellent post-military life for them through multimillion-dollar employment contracts. All they had to do was play the game.

The name of today's game was: how do we scare the shit out of the American people and make them return to the war mongering Republican Party.

'We could fuck around for twenty minutes, or just say it,' Leon Spleetz opened the meeting.

Spleetz could see his war-men were focused. They all knew the game and what was required. There was no need for preamble.

'We have been baiting the Chinese for the past twenty years in the Taiwan Strait and South China Sea,' Sharp-and-Dangerous led the narrative. 'It's American policy to always have a potential conflict brewing somewhere in the world for a rainy day. Look out the window, gentlemen, and you'll see it's raining.'

He knew it was not a great metaphor as they were presently underground.

The Mercurial Blue— DICE

Team Kenny was back onboard the ship, all with horrendous hangovers. Their nightclub party had ended in all manner of shenanigans.

To their credit the team did the night well. After many lessons learned, instead of picking their own clothes they let the shop assistants help them.

The shop people were delighted to help. Picking out clothing options for tall, trim people was a treat. The aliens slid into high-end fashion clothes like a Muskerie stealth penis slid into a warm, hand-rolled Lethantia pastry.

After an excessive number of try-ons, debates and episodes of chronic indecision, Team Kenny were finally fitted-out for their big night out.

'Now let's go get shit-faced!' Rebekah suggested.

She had stumbled across this term while watching a reality TV show starring teenage mums with multiple babies after fornicating with entire high school lacrosse teams. These mums were experts at binge drinking.

'Salute!' Rebekah had told the TV.

'Go girl!' Alicia told her, instantly feeling nauseous for agreeing with anything Rebekah said. 'I need to get fucked up.'

Kenny looked at her with a mix of terror and sexual excitement. Alicia didn't hold back while sober. What the hell would she be like in state of fucked-upness?

He shivered.

One block from the hotel they found a large city bar. It was nearly six o'clock on a Friday night and filled with city office workers looking to blow off some steam before heading back to the suburbs to wives or husbands, screaming kids, shitty Friday night pizza, and Netflix reruns.

As they entered the bar, everyone spun around for a good look at the aliens. Alicia led them in to the bar and ordered tequila shots, putting down a large wad of hundred-dollar bills.

The barman stared at the money.

'Take one for yourself, my man,' she told him. 'And keep the shots coming. In fact, *shots for everyone!*'

The bar suddenly went quiet. It took a few seconds for the revellers to process this recent development. A super-hot chick in a bright white tiny skirt and big black boots had just bought everyone a drink.

The crowd cheered once. They hooted twice. Then skulled the shots.

'Do it again!' Alicia yelled, and the crowd went wild.

Over the next thirty minutes the volume in the bar exceeded healthy noise limits, as the endless supply of Alicia-shots flowed.

People were trying to talk over each other, and the music was cranked all the way up. The revellers, many of whom had no right singing in public, joined in at maximum lung capacity.

Kenny and Kyle attracted the attention of more than a few very tidy ladies, who all seemed intent on getting plastered, then laid, while the Team Kenny girls had men five-deep competing for their attention.

Kenny learnt that wearing white chinos was a mistake, when a very friendly lady in a business suit managed to push her boobs into his chest while lifting her knee onto his crotch. When her knee found what it was looking for, it moved up and down, then side to side.

If not for the discreet indirect lighting, everyone would have seen the front of Kenny's pants impersonating a lighthouse.

He was only used to lasting thirty seconds with Alicia, as this was all she would allow. So he concentrated on Balorgian amateur fish racing and Tiporian glacial swimming.

***

The next morning, Kenny woke up on the floor of the hotel room. It took him a several seconds to untangle himself from under three women. His head buzzed like a chainsaw and his mouth felt like he'd scooped up an acre of Zetarian desert.

As he regained his senses, Kenny heard a scream emanate from Alicia's bedroom and watched two naked men run out clutching their clothes.

'Morning, boys,' Kenny offered as they ran past him.

The men didn't have time for niceties, as they crash-opened the front door, making their escape into the hallway. A second later, Alicia appeared yelling something uncivilised.

'Did you lose something?' Kenny asked her, still sitting on the floor.

She looked down at him.

'Get up and follow me,' she told him.

Kenny started shaking and puked on the floor.

***

It took the GOP, along with their army of surrogates and influencers three days to unravel the hack James had performed. As they attempted to log-in to their social media accounts, the hack recycled and they were back to square one.

Within a month, post-election, the people of America lost all interest in politics. Without the GOP crazies and

Fox News screaming lies night and day, there was nothing to see.

The Democratic House and Senate got on with the job of changing election campaign laws to ban super PACs and unregulated money. Lobbyists were banned from the capitol and organised lobbying itself was outlawed.

In one all-encompassing law, all the nation's billionaires were forced to start paying tax. They dramatically reduced Pentagon spending and pulled troops out of the decades-long wars.

A flood of public money appeared in the federal budget and the national debt was eliminated.

New education bills were voted in. Teachers were placed on high income, incentive based performance programmes. Fully funded universal healthcare was implemented and every food manufacturer who loaded their products with sugar and chemicals was taxed at 80%.

Giant agricultural companies were dragged before congress and fined billions of dollars for their decades of farmer and consumer abuse. Farmers were finally free to farm how nature intended.

All the evil empires were hit; Big Energy, social media companies, medical, pharmaceutical, and the gun industry. All were dragged into a new era of transparency and accountability. Many were regulated and taxed good and hard.

The abundance of new public money was diverted to roads, bridges, and dams. A national high-speed rail programme was initiated, and alternative energy research was heavily funded.

Vast sums of federal dollars were spent on pure research programmes to build smart machines and supercomputers to drive the next generation of artificial intelligence.

America was set to do what it does best: invent things, build things and export things.

***

King Zillian-Zeet analysed these events and became engorged with rage. To let off a little steam, he ordered the public flogging of one hundred peasants.

He desperately wanted to flog his generals for good measure, but knew that was out of the question due to his wife's noodle pulling skills. So flogging people he didn't give a shit about would need to suffice.

'What to do?' he asked himself.

At once the answer came to him.

Zillian may have been a sociopathic lunatic, but he was also a great strategist. His governing principle in all problem solving was to follow the money.

Who on Earth was going to lose out the most by the removal of the US Republican Party, he asked himself. The multi trillion-dollar weapons industry was the clear and undisputed answer.

Zillian Zeet quickly hatched a plan.

'Assemble the generals!' He yelled at his aide.

Zillian seethed with pure contempt as he watched the generals float-hop into his chamber.

'You useless pack of pricks!' he told them. 'Earth's United States has successfully rid itself of right-wing politics. Within a year the whole planet will become civilised like Northern fucking Europe.'

The generals sat in silence, determined to show no outward sign of emotion. This took very little effort for the Zeet as they had no facial features. They just had to sit still and not wriggle.

'This means they'll become candidates for selection into the Galactic Society,' Zillian almost spat. 'No more slave labour trade! No more free beef steaks!'

'What will you have us do, sire?' General Took asked.

'I'll tell you what we're going to do,' Zillian began. 'We're going to start a war on Earth, and it's going to be a big one.'

The generals could only sit and listen. They knew their king was completely beyond reason by this point and their input was neither requested nor desired. They were passengers on a train that was about to hit a mountain.

'Because this mission is far above your collective capacity,' Zillian continued, 'I will lead it myself. You will set up defences here at home in case it all goes tits up.'

Silence.

'Now get the fuck out!' the king ordered his generals.

'Get my cruiser ready,' he told his aide.

As all technologically developed worlds in the universe knew, the void between celestial bodies in the universe is far from empty.

As the great professor of Intergalactic Immersed Energy, a one Leonard B. Giggalore, liked to say in his trigennial post-graduate science academy parties: 'The whole fucking thing, from toes to tits, is an interconnected mass of vibrating electromagnetic radiation. As such, it's tailor-made for near instant inter-galactic travel.'

Professor Giggalore, being a massive bag of hot air, loved the sound of his own voice. Once he got on a roll, you simply couldn't shut the bastard up.

'Anti-gravity,' he went on. 'Came about when a craft was set to vibrate at a specific range of frequencies. When harmonic resonance is achieved, a craft, no matter its size and weight, becomes one with the universal energy field and time stops.'

He was not quite done, as two or three people were still listening to him.

'While in this state of harmonic resonance, it is possible to accelerate to unlimited velocities that dwarf the speed of light, for as long as required, without using more than a few thousand watts of power fed into ion-engines.

In practical terms, Zillian-Zeet reached Earth's solar system in one hour, and most of that time was spent pissing about with space port undocking and manoeuvring.

Once again, the Zeet mission needed to be highly covert. If the Seabertian observation ship spotted them, the game was up. Zeet employed the same tactics as before and approached Earth from behind the moon.

As the moon orbited the Earth, it gave his cruiser the cover it needed. He then approached the planet from the opposite side to the *Mercurial Blue*.

'Good flying,' Zillian Zeet told his first officer. 'Place us in stationary orbit right here.' Zillian ordered by placing his tiny finger on a the holgraphic map.

As the ship slowed and settled into its stable orbit, Zillian checked his notes.

'Our data tells us Leo Spleetz is their head weapons manufacturer. Find him, Number One!' Zillian commanded.

Finding one Earthling amongst eight billion may have seemed a challenge, but the Zeet had already hacked into Earth's StarLight telecommunications network and found Spleetz's cell phone frequency code.

'He's here, sir!' Number One said, illuminating at a spot on the holographic map.

'Go get him!' Zillian said firmly with a huge smile. This was fun, he told himself. He missed the good old days when he was a mass-abductor. He loved the way Earthlings tried to scream but couldn't move their mouths. All that begging and pleading to let them go excited Zillian Zeet to no end.

Several thousand miles below, on earth, (fill the gap)Leo Spleetz had finished work for the day and was driving back to his three-storey Long Island beach home. It was a special night for his family.

His wife had done something for a charity that raised a huge amount of l money for a cause he couldn't give a shit about.

The point was, his wife was twenty-five years old and recently crowned Miss Romania. In one week, her YouTube yoga channel received over five million hits. What could he say? The woman liked exercising in see-through leggings that showed off her perfect arse.

Spleetz thought about her arse and was rewarded with a huge pants chub.

His chub, however, was about to die a rapid death as his whole world became illuminated in blinding white light.

He was so shocked, he hit the gas instead of the brake and his V-12 Bentley accelerated beyond the Zeet light field. Now in pitch black, and blind from the light, Spleetz drove off the road and hit a tree.

'What the fuck is this idiot doing?' The Zeet abduction team leader yelled, viewing the wreck. 'Get the light back on his car.'

As Spleetz's Bentley hit the tree, a bunch of airbags wrapped Spleetz up in a cocoon before anything pointy could touch him. The impact transformed the passenger compartment into a protective cage and unhinged his door, where Leo Spleetz tumbled out onto the ground.

'Okay, boys, watch this. Ten to one he does the chicken run.'

The Zeet guessed right.

Spleetz looked up into the light, then started running left, then right, then left again.

'Hit him with the gun.'

A Zeet aimed a laser pointer at Spleetz and then shot him with a phaser beam. Spleetz collapsed mid-stride and tumbled like a Jell-O ball.

'Let's go get him,' the team leader ordered and did the universal whirly motion with his flimsy hand.

Thirty minutes later, Leo Spleetz was coming around inside the Zeet star cruiser, and he didn't like what he saw.

Being one of the most powerful men on planet Earth, Spleetz acted exactly as expected and yelled at his captors. At least he thought he was yelling, but no sound came out.

He then felt a sharp pain deep inside his head.

It was an old Zeetian trick to zap a belligerent abductee to shut them up and gain their focus. When the pain stopped, Spleetz heard a voice inside his mind, as clearly as though someone was speaking.

'Leo, please relax. We are not here to hurt you,' the voice told him. It took Spleetz a second, but he quickly recognised the speaker. It was Charlize Theron. Spleetz had met Charlize once at a charity do, where she told him not to touch her.

'Charlize?' Spleetz asked. 'What the fuck are you doing here?'

'I'm not really Charlize. I just thought this voice would be more comforting for you,' the mind-voice told him.

Spleetz finally realised he was having a stroke and his mind had gone on some kind of freaky pre-death bender. He decided not to engage with Charlize and let whatever was going to happen, just happen already.

'Leo,' the voice continued, 'you are in an alien spaceship and we are your friends.'

Spleetz looked around at the interior of the ship and shuddered.

'We know that your Republican political protectors have been voted out of office. We are here to help you regain your power,' fake Charlize told him in her deep, soothing voice. 'It's very important that we speak. If we let you sit up do you promise not to panic? No more chicken running, okay?'

No more chicken running? What the fuck? Spleetz thought. *Maybe this is actually happening.*

'Good!' Fake Charlize said. 'You can sit up now.'

All at once, Spleetz felt he could move his body again. He moved his arms and legs and raised his head.

'Oh, fuck my Jesus!' He yelled as Zillian Zeet came into view. 'They really do look like that!'

'Not they, Leo,' fake Charlize said. 'We.'

Leo Spleetz passed out on his own accord this time.

By the time Spleetz awoke, Zillian had brain transferred him. He was now fully cognisant of the situation and ready to communicate with his captors.

Time was not an issue either, as the Zeet ship remained in time-pause harmonisation mode.

Zillian Zeet and Leo Spleetz spoke for an hour via their mental bridge. By the end of the meeting they had reached an agreement and a plan was hatched.

The pair of despot sociopaths developed a multifaceted scheme to create havoc on Earth and restore Republican political insanity back to the United States.

'We're going to send you home now,' fake Charlize told Spleetz. 'Sorry about the tree thing and your broken car. I'm told Bentlys are really cool cars. I'd get one myself, but I can't reach the peddles. Besides, the rest of galaxy stopped using cars eons ago. We travel by hover bubbles now. Oh, and by the way, I've already had the abduction team flogged.'

'Good,' Spleetz replied. 'Can you tell the real Charlize to call me?'

'I don't think that's a good idea, Spleetz. She thinks you're a bit of a dick,' the fake Charlize told him.

'Fair enough,' a dejected Spleetz sighed.

Five minutes later, he woke up on the ground next to his crumpled car. The car had sent off an emergency message upon impact, and Spleetz could already hear sirens approaching.

Thirty minutes after that, he was in his home drinking some very expensive pinot red wine that he imported from New Zealand of all places.

'Where the hell is New Zealand? Many of his friends had asked.

'How the fuck should I know!' Spleetz told them. 'It's the home of great pinot, I guess.'

He could hear his Romanian wife jabbering on in her grating Count Dracula accent but couldn't hear a word she was saying.

All he could think about was Charlize Theron and the massive chub in his pants.

Three weeks later...

Chairman of the Senate Arms Committee, Senator Linus J. Humber, sat down to lunch with his favourite nephew, navy captain Reese Humber.

They were joined by a third man Reese Humber had never met. The man had a sharp and dangerous look about him.

'Gerry Gall, meet my nephew, Captain Reese Humber,' the senator said, then turned to a waiter and ordered coffees.

Reese Humber had never met a man who failed to match his name quite like Sharp-and-Dangerous.

'Gerry works for a military contractor. Sorry, I can't tell you which one,' the senator announced. 'All I can say is, it has a lot to do with top secret weapons testing.'

Reese Humber was fine with that. He was a forty-year-old captain of an ultra-modern Virginia class nuclear submarine. As such, he lived in a world of secrets and need-to-know security structures.

'As you have read in your briefing papers, the Chinese are becoming highly bolshy in and around Taiwan,' the senator told his nephew. 'This is of grave concern to the Pentagon.'

The waiter arrived with coffee.

'If the Democratic White House has its way, and we do nothing, China will invade Taiwan,' the senator continued.

Captain Reese had practised hundreds of war-game exercises against China in that region. All concluded with the release of nuclear weapons. If it even looked like American submarines would dominate Chinese home waters, they would fire their nuclear torpedoes.

'We live in dangerous times, Reese,' the senator told him. 'If we don't flex our muscles now, it may be too late.'

Reese nodded. He loved and respected his uncle. He believed him to be the last bastion of US military strength and would follow him down any path.

'May I?' Gerry asked the senator.

'Go ahead.'

'Captain Humber, we need your help,' Gerry began. 'We need you to tweak the tail of the dragon.'

Meanwhile... on the planet Zeet

General Coleus Zeet called a secret meeting with General Zeus Zeet. Both of these men were unremarkable in many ways. Yet, they were of sound mind enough to know the current operation on planet Earth was going to end in tears.

They also knew it was impossible for a galactic power to initiate a war between two Earth-bound civilisations, especially for the purpose of profit, and get away with it.

It was time to hang Zillian Zeet by the feet and shoot him full of arrows, this being the traditional method of execution for shitbag kings on the planet Zeet.

'Do you have a plan?' Coleus Zeet asked, as planning was not his strong point.

'I have the start of one,' Zeus Zeet told him. 'But we must not have our fingerprints anywhere near this.'

Both men nodded and drank some Floog tea. The tea was renowned for the treatment of Zeetian grawl worms which had plagued their species from the day they stole the planet from the Yipes.

The Yipes, in their final act of revenge against marauding Zeet hoards, genetically modified the prolific grawl worm and turned it lose. The worms spread across the planet like brush fire, entering, then clinging to the Zeetian gut lining like a rock climber who forgot to pack his safety ropes.

'Fuck, this tea sucks,' Coleus said and spat out a piece of leaf.

Zeus took another sip and shook his head in disgust.

'It really does,' he announced. 'Okay, this is how I want to do it.'

Three days later, a Zeet deep-space resupply drone commenced its slowdown procedure as it approached the dark side of Earth's moon.

As it neared the moon-approach waypoint, the original flight programme shut down and the drone shuddered. Five-tenths of a second later, a new programme booted-up and the drone continued its voyage.

Now the drone was on a very different mission. Instead of turning right, and heading toward the Zeet star cruiser, it hooked left and flew toward the *Mercurial Blue*.

On the flight bridge of the *Blue*, the flight deck duty officer was working her way through a particularly frustrating Seabertian sudoku puzzle when a proximity alarm made her drop her space pencil.

'What the hell!' She said loudly enough to gain the crew's attention. 'Why is there a spacecraft heading toward us? Are we expecting visitors?'

The crew stood and silently watched their screen.

'Nothing on the schedule,' someone declared.

'Hail the ship!' She commanded. 'Weapons officer! Track and lock this fucker!'

Both the communications and weapons officers went to work as the drone flew on, directly toward them. It then began transmitting a Zeet communication code.

'Zeets! Hit it with a targeting beam!' The duty officer commanded. The targeting beam was a powerful electrical pulse used for weapon guidance. It basically told the target ship it was about to be blown into space junk.

The drone ignored the signal.

The duty officer called colonel Hipu.

'We have a Zeet transport on our bearing. It's coming in hot and not responding to our hails or target tracking.'

'If it closes to five hundred miles, destroy it.' Hipu ordered. He was very excited and ran toward the bridge as fast as his heavy legs would carry him.

Colonel Hipu realised he hadn't killed anyone in years and this was his chance to break the drought. He was so excited, in fact, he forgot to take a pre-combat pee pee.

Seconds later, he reached the bridge.

'Status report!' Hipu ordered, taking up his seat in the captain's chair.

'Sir! It's a Zeet transport drone. Range one thousand miles and closing, but it appears to slowing down.'

Hipu ran through a menu of possible options and knew that all of them sucked. What the hell could a Zeet drone be doing out here?

'Sir,' the communications officer said. 'The drone is sending a message in galactic military code. Wait one. Okay, it's saying: "Don't kill me. I carry vital information".'

'Don't fucking kill me! Bullshit! Kill it once it breaks five hundred miles!' the colonel ordered.

'Sir, the drone has stopped. Range seven hundred miles,' the duty officer announced.

The colonel gave himself time to think. Someone had gone to a lot of trouble in sending this thing out here. What could he lose by taking a look? *Opportunity or threat?* the colonel mused. *Time will tell.*

'Send out one of our drones and plug a line into it. If it so much as twitches, blow it to hell.'

Twenty minutes later the Seabertian drone docked with the Zeet ship.

The *Mercurial Blue* flight officers watched as the two craft joined in space. Within seconds a transmission was being broadcast onto the *Blue*'s main monitor.

Zeus Zeet had videoed the king's instructions to assault Earth and it appeared in 12k clarity on the big TV.

The colonel sat back into his captain's chair and scratched his woolly hair. *This day just went from zero to 1000 parsecs in three wartums*, he mused.

'Comms, get me the admiral!'

Admiral Gustov sat passively while Colonel Hipu ran through recent events.

'What are your orders, sir?' Colonel Hipu asked.

Admiral Gustov thought for a moment.

'This has all the makings for a major diplomatic disaster. Catching Zillian Zeet red-handed in the middle of a massive crime is delicate stuff. We need to be very careful how we handle it,' he told Colonel Hipu.

The admiral had a long and contemptuous history with the Zeets. He personally hated the clammy little grey bastards. There were many things he'd like to do right now, but he also knew there was only one legal action available to him.

'Colonel Hipu,' he began, 'we must assume there is a Zeet star cruiser on the other side of Earth. Take your ship out into deep space and come back in behind him. Have your weapons on stand-by, but don't lock-on. The last thing you want is a fight with a star cruiser. Just take it easy.'

'Yes, Admiral,' Hipu replied, and nodded to his navigator.

'When you are on the other side,' the admiral continued. 'I will do the talking.'

'Copy, sir,' Hipu said.

The *Mercurial Blue* was a stealthy ship and was not noticed as it came around to the other side of Earth. The crew found the Zeet star cruiser in a matter of minutes.

'There she is,' the colonel announced. 'Bold as brass!'

A few minutes after they reached the desired position, a communication signal was beamed to the Zeet star cruiser.

Zillian Zeet nearly jumped out of his tiny spacesuit as the image of Admiral Gustov appeared on the main screen. In that fraction of a second he knew he was done.

Yet, being a famous galactic narcissist, sociopath and liar, Zillian Zeet decided to hold his ground as he worked through his range of options.

If he vaporised the Seabertian ship, would anyone know it was him? *Of course, they would—there's a live signal link back to Space Corp. Fuck!*

Do they actually know we're in the middle of a crime? Why else would they be here? Double Fuck! Can I just hit the hyper-drive and run? That would buy some time for me to create a story...

'Zillian Zeet!' The admiral boomed. 'One of your drones has up-loaded your plans to start a war on Earth.'

Zillian shuddered.

'Under the authority vested in me under Galactic law nine-eight-seven-two-four-seven-one, (Close the gap) being the unsanctioned sedition and active engagement in armed conflict on a foreign world, I am placing you under arrest.'

'Sir! They're heating up!' The duty officer yelled.

'Zeet! *Don't do it*!' The admiral yelled.

Too late.

Zillian Zeet punched his hyperdrive engine, creating a massive hole in the local electromagnet energy field and the star cruiser disappeared.

Entering hyperspace in close proximity to another spacecraft has a devastating effect. The event causes a temporary vacuum in the EM field, much like a small black hole, or singularity.

The *Mercurial Blue* was plunged into the EM hole, and a number of very bad things happened all at once. The ship lost all electrical power and spun through the vacuum vortex like a bug flushed down a drain.

With the loss of electrical power, the ship's artificial gravity failed and the crew were tossed about like rag dolls.

On Earth, the EM blast blew out every electrical fuse and breaker in Europe, Africa and half of Western Asia.

Commander Kenny and Lieutenant Alicia, who by this stage were pretty much boyfriend and girlfriend, were tossed out of bed and bounced around their cabin a few times before coming to rest on the deck in pitch darkness.

'That's not good,' Kenny told Alicia, whose tits were pushed deep into his face.

'What in all fuckness just happened?' She asked with no real expectation of a credible answer.

One second later, the *Blue* was hit again as a massive force of electromagnet energy surged back into the void.

As the ship tumbled, over and over, the crew and their onboard machines were thrust together for a second time, then darkness overcame them. As the alarms rang out, the real terror began.

Crew members who remained conscious had no idea if the hull was breached, or if the ship was tumbling toward the surface of the earth.

To them, it appeared all was lost.

Minutes later, the ship's computers re-booted, lights flickered a few times then came back on, quickly joined by the ship's artificial gravity. Everything and everyone who was floating in space, fell back to the floor hard.

Kenny unburied his face from Alicia's chest and crawled toward the cabin door. Realising it was safe to stand, he opened the door and raced toward the command bridge with Alicia close behind.

Along the way, they saw many of the crew lying crumpled on the deck. Some had open head wounds and broken limbs. Kenny knew he must remain focused. He was a senior officer of the ship and had to reach the bridge.

'I have to—' he began.

'You go,' Alicia told him. 'I'll help out here.'

Kenny nodded and kept running.

He got to the bridge and found complete chaos. Half the crew were still on the deck. Everyone not unconscious had some kind of injury. They were all dazed and non-operational.

He then found Colonel Hipu. He was on the deck between his captain's chair and a navigation console with a deep six-inch cut running down the middle of his head. He was not moving and his eyes were wide open.

'Communications officer!' Kenny yelled into the room. He looked from face to face, hoping someone would recover enough to start performing.

'*People*!' Kenny yelled, hurting his own head. 'I need you to function! Who's my comms officer?'

A young lieutenant with a badly broken arm and blood seeping from a head wound put his good arm up.

Kenny looked around and found the medical box. He opened it and pulled out a bandage and a painkiller huffer. He quickly treated the man's head and made a sling for his arm.

'Puff on this this,' Kenny told him. The huffer contained morphine and amphetamines, a good mix for combat pain relief.

Kenny also took a hit.

'Can you function?' Kenny asked him, and the comms officer nodded.

'Good. Get me a damage report and connect me to engineering, ASAP!' Kenny ordered him.

As the comms officer went to work, Kenny continued applying first aid to another wounded crew member.

'Commander! I have engineering on screen-one,' the comms officer announced.

'What have we got, Chief?' Kenny asked a man who looked like train-wreck survivor.

'Fucking Zeets hit their hyperdrive right on top of us,' the chief engineer said, as he wiped some blood off his mouth. 'They blew out our main electrical board and scrammed the reactor.'

'Are we operational?' Kenny asked.

'Right now, we have life-support and gravity on emergency power. We are working to get the reactor back, but that won't happen until I have tested the cooling system from end to end. Most of my team are injured and I have three fatalities. Can you get medical down here?'

Kenny triaged the needs of the ship, and engineering came first. *Without them, we all die*, he told himself.

'I'll have a med-team to you ASAP. Hang tough, Chief,' Kenny told him.

'Navigator!' Kenny called. 'Get me our position, heading and velocity.'

Kenny sat down in the captain's chair for a moment. It was only then he felt warm blood seeping down the back of his neck. He felt around and discovered a huge gash on his head.

He reached into his jacket and pulled out his communicator. To his surprise it wasn't broken, so he called Alicia.

'Engineering needs help. They're busted up down there. Can you muster a med team?' Kenny said.

Kenny thanked the Gods she was tough and good in a crisis. If anyone could get them help, it was her.

'I'll be there in there in two minutes,' Alicia told him.

Piece by piece, the ship's systems came back online and communications were restored to Admiral Gustov.

Kenny read out the damage report and gave him the casualty list.

Amongst the dead was Colonel Hipu.

Kenny checked and discovered that James, along with the three ensigns, was fine. Just a few cuts and bruises but there was a lot of complaining coming from Rebekah, whose fart rabbit was dead.

'Lieutenant Commander Kendrick, you have done well restoring command of the ship,' the admiral told him. 'As you are senior officer, I'm making you a full commander. The ship is yours.'

Kenny paused while that development resonated through his hazy brain. He nodded and thought, *Fuck it! Here we go then!*

'What are your orders, sir?' Kenny asked. He was still too sore and concussed to be pleased with his promotion. It was like living through a bad dream.

'Restore full power. Muster all your remaining functioning crew and brief them. There must be a lot of confusion onboard. Then re-position the ship in stable Earth orbit. Once you're done, contact me for further instructions,' the admiral told him. 'Look after your ship and people now, son.'

'Thank you, Admiral. *Mercurial Blue* standing by.' Kenny signed off, and got to work.

USS New Jersey: Virginia Class nuclear-powered fast-attack submarine
Captain Reese Humber commanding, somewhere in the Taiwan Strait

Reese's mission plan originated in the Department of the Navy, was passed onto the Pentagon, then came directly to Reese from the director of Naval Operations.

It was finally placed in the captain's safe onboard the *USS New Jersey*.

At 0400 Taiwan time, a secure message was sent to the New Jersey. The message was decoded by a senior radio chief, then sealed and handed to Humber in his cabin.

EYES ONLYTOP SECRET***

Take the New Jersey 50 miles off the port city of Xiamen, China. Once you arrive open your sealed orders. When your mission is completed, make your way back to Hawaii undetected by the safest possible route. It is essential you leave no trace of your presence.

Director Naval Operations
END MESSAGE

***

Aboard the *Mercurial Blue*, most of the ship's departments were back online and full electrical power was restored.

'Get me the admiral,' Kenny ordered. Almost immediately the reassuring face of Admiral Gustov appeared on screen.

'Status report,' the admiral asked.

'We are operational, sir,' Kenny told him.

'Well done, Commander. Now we have to find out what those arsehole Zeets were focused on,' the admiral said. 'Whatever they were doing can't be good.'

'Sir, we have intercepted a worrying military signal just sent to a US nuclear submarine operating in the Strait of Taiwan,' Kenny reported. 'The sub has been sent to a position off the port city of Xiamen, and the captain was told to open his secret orders. Obviously, we don't know what they are.'

'Our intelligence people have been working on this,' the admiral told him. ''When Zeet mischief is afoot, the answer is always about money. We ran several computer simulations and the most logical outcome is that the Zeet have made a deal with the American military to restore the Republican Party back into power. The only way they can make this can happen is to start a war.'

'Because without their Republican party, the military and the Zeet lose,' Kenny surmised.

'Correct,' the admiral told him.

'Do we intervene?' Kenny asked.

'Commander Kendrick, it was you who created this mess, so you may as well finish it.' The admiral smiled and winked at him.

Kenny viewed the admiral's wink and got a warm fuzzy feeling all over. He had broken all the eggs, now it was time to make his omelette.

He took another huff of pain killer and amthamines, then went to work.

Seabertian transport craft onboard the *Mercurial Blue* were all multi-elemental. They were built to travel through space, air, and just as efficiently through water. In fact, they made for kick-arse submarines when that task was required.

Kenny held a briefing with *Mercurial Blue*'s abduction team leader, Lieutenant Rick, and his second in command, Sergeant Lisa. The abduction team members were all fully trained special operations military, but rarely used for actual combat.

Both Rick and Lisa were ecstatic to have the chance to kick some arse.

'I want you to take Lieutenant Alicia,' Kenny told them. 'She will be my comms officer for this mission.'

Rick and Lisa looked at Alicia, who returned their stare with a "don't fuck with me" attitude.

'Fair enough,' Rick told Kenny.

With their mission in hand, the team strapped themselves into a transport and launched through the transit dock toward planet Earth.

***

The *USS New Jersey* had reached her assigned position off the Chinese coast just fifty miles from Xiamen.

Captain Humber left the command centre and entered his cabin. There, he opened the safe and removed his encoded orders.

Using his "Eye's Only" decoding card, Humber read the orders.

You are to remain in position off the coast of Xiamen and maintain a silent presence. There you will attempt to track any Chinese military surface or submerged vessel that emerges from the port. Once you have identified a target you are to track it beyond 30 miles from the Chinese coast then engage the vessel using active targeting sonar. You are to then to launch your noise-maker countermeasures and escape at high-speed heading southeast, clear of the area. The rules of engagement are: if you are fired upon, you may return fire with whatever weapons system you deem appropriate for the survival of your boat. END

Captain Humber read the orders twice more, then placed the document back into the safe and locked it.

He knew exactly what the Chinese ship would do once it was hit by a targeting sonar ping.

It would drop counter measures, come-about, find his boat and launch torpedoes. Humber would then have no choice but to manoeuvre, then fire his own torpedoes.

All this would occur in Chinese waters and would be deemed to be an act of war.

So, this is it, he told himself. *I'm about to start World War Three.*

***

Lieutenant Rick knew the location of the New Jersey and plunged the transport into the sea fifty miles from the boat. Seabertian underwater detection sensors were several thousands of years more advanced than those onboard the *USS New Jersey*.

It didn't take long for Rick to find her.

'Look at that fat fucker,' he told his team. 'This is going to be fun.'

The Seabertian craft hovered in the *New Jersey*'s baffles, well behind her propellors, and waited.

Alicia was about to pour a cup of coffee. Not olikian, of course, as that was banned on combat missions. Horny and homicidal were mutually exclusive, or so deemed the war committee. There was no room for randy soldiers in deep space combat, the handbook stated.

'Don't drink that,' Rick told her. 'We may be here for a while and I don't want you pissing in my ship.'

Alicia wanted to stab Rick in the heart with her shiny new combat knife, but knew that would cause too much fuss. She resealed the coffee flask and sighed.

An hour passed. Then another.

'Bless, my greasy ort!' Alicia complained. 'What are these motherfuckers doing?'

'Shush!' Rick told her.

Alicia placed her hand on the knife. *One more time, Pissy Rick*, she said to herself. *Just one more fucking time.*

'We have movement,' Sergeant Lisa announced.

All eyes went to the main display screen. Their sensors showed a ship leaving the port.

'Plant and propellors sound military,' Lisa told them.

The same report came to Captain Humber on the *New Jersey*.

Humber had positioned himself in the command centre and was ready for action.

'Okay, set up your track and wait for them to go by,' he ordered.

Over the next hour, both the Seabertians and the Americans tracked the Chinese warship. It was a modern destroyer of around 8000 tons. *A nice juicy prize*, Humber told himself.

The Chinese ship was not using active sonar this close to shore. The Americans were never stupid enough to position themselves off a naval base, or so the Chinese captain reasoned.

The destroyer clipped out of port at a tidy 15 knots; she then turned left on a heading of 30 degrees north-east into the Taiwan Strait.

The American boat allowed her to pass by, then turned to follow.

'Okay,' Rick said. 'Time for some fun. Give her plenty of room, Lisa.'

While the American boat focused on the Chinese destroyer, the Seabertian transport worked her way to within 300 feet of her stern. Lisa positioned them behind and a little to the left of the sub to avoid the propeller wash.

'Okeydokey then,' Lieutenant Rick affirmed. 'Hook us up.'

Alicia stared at Rick with renewed contempt. What sort of inbreed, cow-fucking hick-talk was "okeydokey"?

Lisa worked her console for a few seconds.

'Standing by,' she announced.

'Launch,' Rick told her.

A small drone left the Seabertian ship and raced toward the *USS New Jersey*. It snaked around the stern of the American boat and aimed for the centre of the hull, just under the sail. With a short loud smack, the drone attached itself to the hull.

Lisa touched another button, triggering a complex array of electronic pulse frequencies that simultaneously froze the New Jersey's manoeuvring controls and disabled her weapons systems.

'What the fuck was that!' Captain Humber yelled. He had heard the worst sound an American sub captain could hear in combat. An unknown object had just hit his hull.

Then someone was talking to him.

'Attention Captain Humber of the *USS New Jersey*. Do not be alarmed and make no sudden moves,' Lieutenant Rick told the American boat.

'Chief!' Humber yelled. 'Crash the boat! Emergency dive! Come right ninety degrees and launch the counter measures.'

The chief relayed the captain's orders, but the submarine remained on its current course and depth.

'Crash the boat, Chief!' Humber yelled again.

'I have disabled your vessel, Captain,' Rick said over the boat's speakers. 'You are not in danger. Please remain calm and do what I say.'

Humber ran to the *Jersey*'s manoeuvring control station. He saw the sailors were attempting to steer the ship but the controls were not responding.

In a state of complete horror, Captain Humber finally realised he had lost control of his boat. Someone, who spoke English with an American accent, had taken over.

He ran through his range of options, but no logical possibilities came to him. No navy, that he knew of, had the technology to creep up on, and then disable an American front-line submarine.

The procedure for surrendering a nuclear submarine to an enemy combatant was not taught at the Naval Academy, yet on this day, deep in enemy waters, Captain Humber was forced to make a decision.

'Who the hell are you, and what do you want?' He demanded.

'Who we are is irrelevant. What we want is for you to set a new course of ninety degrees east and submerge to five hundred feet. You must exit the Taiwan Strait immediately. If you comply, I will release your boat.'

Humber performed another status analysis. He was a good chess player, but had no move to play.

'Chief! Status report,' he demanded.

'No change, sir. We're still locked up,' the chief told him.

Humber viewed his crew. He could see they were all scared and confused. Their training began and ended with using America's most powerful weapon system to defeat all her enemies. Not this shit.

Humber made the most painful decision of his life and capitulated to a foe he could not see or fight.

'Prepare to come right. Make your heading ninety degrees east and submerge to five hundred feet,' Humber said in a small, hollow voice.

'Very well, Captain,' Rick told him. 'Your ship is released.'

With that, the Seabertian drone sent a new pulse through the submarine. Within seconds, the *Jersey* turned right and went deep.

'What about the drone?' Lisa asked.

'Leave it on for a little longer,' Rick told her.

Alicia flopped back in her chair.

'Looks like we're not killing anyone today,' she sighed.

Rick and Lisa turned and stared at her.

'What?' Alicia asked them. Captain Humber entertained the idea of revenge by turning back to engage whatever the hell it was that disabled his boat. Yet logic prevailed. He needed to end this nightmare as quickly and calmly as possible.

Once well clear of the Chinese ship, the *Jersey* increased speed to forty knots, on a direct course for Pearl Harbour.

The Seabertians followed him for another hour until Rick was satisfied.

'Okay, lose the drone,' he told Lisa. 'Then take us back to the *Blue*.'

***

On the command deck of the *Mercurial Blue*, Kenny, the admiral, along with over one trillion homes across the galaxy, watched the entire event unfold.

Geon Plume and Todd Splick knew the award for best drama was in the bag as they took a new raft of multi-million murk sponsorship offers.

'Well, that worked!' the admiral told Kenny.

'It sure as fuck did! Oops, sorry, sir,' Kenny apologised for his potty mouth.

'That's okay, son,' the admiral told him.

Kenny, wanted to hug the admiral, as he really missed his real dad.

'I have to go now,' the admiral told Kenny. 'I need to write up a list of charges against the Zillian Zeet and arrest him.'

'Good luck, sir! I Hope you nail the arse-probing bastard!' Kenny told him.

'Keep a tight eye on these American military bastards,' the admiral told him. 'Call me if they try something else.'

'Copy that, sir,' Kenny affirmed. 'We'll double our intercept surveillance.'

***

Three days later, the *USS New Jersey* approached submarine pen number nine at the Pearl Harbour Naval Base.

Waiting at the dock was Captain Reese Humber's uncle, Senator Humber. With him were two admirals and Gerry, who looked sharper and more dangerous than ever.

The young captain knew this wasn't to be a cheery greeting.

All the navy knew was that the *Jersey* had cut short her mission and was returning home. Then the *Jersey* stopped broadcasting.

Humber docked his boat, grabbed his bags, and walked down the gangplank as soon as it was laid.

How appropriate, he thought, as he walked the plank.

Without a word of a greeting, the men on the dock turned and walked toward an awaiting van, with Captain Humber trailing.

The van door slammed shut, and before Humber was fully seated, the admiral was speaking.

'What the hell happened out there?'

Captain Humber numbly stared back at the man for longer than the admiral could wait.

'Well?' He asked sharply.

Humber gave a little cough.

'I opened my orders and took up my position. We were following a Chinese destroyer, as per our orders, when—'

'When what?' Senator Humber demanded.

'When an unknown craft made contact with my boat. It attached an unknown object on to our hull. It must have been some kind of communications device. It disabled my boat and started giving me instructions. We lost all capacity to manoeuvre the boat, and our weapons systems were disabled.'

Captain Humber was starting to sweat and his hands were shaking.

The admiral pulled out his phone and dialled a pre-set number.

'Detain the crew,' he told whoever answered. 'No, on the boat! Keep them on the boat. No visitors, and no calls in or out. Shut down all comms and get the tapes. No, I mean all the fucking tapes for the whole sortie. Then lock them in my safe. Eyes only from here on in.'

The Admiral closed his phone and focused back on Captain Humber.

'Give us the details,' the Admiral commanded.

'Whatever attacked us, it managed to approach my boat in complete silence then disable us. The voice said to disengage from the destroyer and return to base. It said we would not get control of the boat again until we complied.'

'What condition were you in?' The admiral asked.

'We were trailing the Chinese destroyer at a range of one thousand yards, and a depth of three hundred feet. We ran at one-third reactor, low-prop cavitation, and were silent. The towed sonar array was deployed, and all our sonars were operating normally.'

The admiral considered this. No mistakes or anomalies there. Everything was by the book, he judged.

'At any point did your sonar get a hit from another craft, besides the destroyer?'

'No, sir,' Humber told him. 'Just the destroyer, and I doubt the drone came from there, as it was doing fifteen knots from our bow and heading away.'

'What did the voice sound like? Was there any kind of accent?' The admiral asked.

'The voice sounded like us,' Humber said. 'American, male, possibly thirty to forty years old. Just slightly different.'

'Canadian?' The Admiral asked.

'No. Like someone who spoke educated American English, but had spent time overseas,' Humber tried his best to explain.

'What does that mean? Which country?' The admiral was losing patience.

'Sorry, I'm not being very helpful. Can I take off my jacket?' Humber was red-faced and sweating hard.

'Okay, I've heard enough,' the admiral announced. 'Now listen up, Captain. Your ship was not attacked. You did not hear voices. You had a high temperature reading in your reactor and you deemed the situation unsafe to continue your mission. And of course, you were nowhere near the Chinese coast.'

Captain Humber was now ready to be arrested. He had committed a naval sin that no one, including nephews of senators, recovered from.

Instead, they drove him and the senator to the naval officer's R&R hotel. Captain Humber watched the van drive away in a state of confusion.

'What will happen now? What about my boat?' he asked.

'Nothing happens now. Your boat suffered a malfunction,' the senator told him. 'Tomorrow you'll oversee the technicians as they examine her. There they'll find a faulty temperature sensor and a software glitch. You'll be reunited with your crew, who are all being debriefed as we speak.'

Captain Humber still looked confused.

'It's okay, my boy. Your crew are being told this was a top secret exercise,' the senator told him. 'That we tested a new weapons system on the *Jersey*. They'll be fine.'

Captain Humber thought about this for a second and nodded.

'Let's get a drink,' the senator told his nephew.

'Well? What was it? What attacked my boat?' Captain Humber asked the older man.

'Son, you wouldn't believe me if I told you.'

'I am a combat naval officer,' Captain Humber said. 'Don't you think I have the right to know the capacity of my enemy?'

'Your "enemy" as you put it, has no equal,' the senator told him. 'You were not attacked by the Russians or the Chinese.'

Reese Humber had heard all the stories of unknown, ultra high-tech underwater craft. Some of his friends had actually seen them.

'Let's get that drink before you completely unspool,' the senator said, and gave the younger man a wink.

'Hang on a minute! Does this mean they,' Humber pointed up to the sky, 'just stopped me from starting a war with China?'

The senator shrugged.

'Looks that way now, doesn't it? Mind you, it's not the first time, even the fourth or fifth. I've read dozens of military reports describing "unknown craft" sightings in and around our bases, crashing our weapons systems. In fact, these reports go back to World War Two.'

Reese Humber's universe suddenly became broader and much deeper.

Planet Zeet

General Coleus Zeet, and General Zeus Zeet, monitored Zillian Zeet's mission in real time from the Military Information and Logistics Facility (MILF).

The generals watched in horror as their king committed the duel galactic crimes of Interplanetary Conspiracy to Incite War and the premeditated assault on a peaceful Star Corp starship.

'This is the final straw! Zeetland has endured much suffering under his rule, but this time Zillian has gone too far. It's time to initiate our coup,' Zeus announced.

Coleus and Zeus rounded up the other generals and laid down the crimes against their king. Once the debate was over and all the questions answered, they submitted their plans for the final coup d'état.

'It is quite clear,' Zeus began. 'If we do nothing, we will be judged as co-conspirators by the Galactic Council. Without a formal leadership structure, Zeetland could fall under their stewardship.'

The generals stared back at him. A coup attempt against Zillian Zeet was no trivial matter. They knew the man as a homicidal manic with a sixth sense for traitorous activities.

To balance this fact, they also knew the League of Galactic Nations would send an armada to the Zeet planet and arrest Zillian anyway. Logic being, if the Zeet generals arrested Zillian, they could come out of this shit-storm without losing too much skin.

As a side benefit, they reasoned, they'd be rid of Zillian once and for all.

'I can see by your faces you have reached the only logical conclusion,' Zeus said.

This was no mean feat, as the Zeet had no facial features.

'It is easy to make bold statements, Zeus. But how do we do this? A coup on this scale against a king like Zillian is no small matter,' General Zorb asked. They all knew Zorb Zeet to be the prick's-prick and nobody liked him.

'We took a bearing from Zillian's cruiser before he disabled his transponder. We believe he's headed to the outer rim of the Nug system,' Zeus told the generals.

'The Nug system! My Gods,' General Klese announced. Klese was the reputed expert on the outer worlds. 'There are forest planets out there you could hide entire armies in.'

'Correct, General Klese,' Zeus told him. 'We have analysed the possible planets where Zillian may hole up. The most promising is BeSkor. It is a goldilocks planet with a suitable atmosphere, habitable temperatures, and the gravity isn't too strong. It orbits around a yellow star called K-TK-nine-nine-seven-Q.'

He activated a holographic map that showed the star and planet.

'Hey! I know this planet,' Klese said. 'It was owned by the rock star Ludie-Lude. Apparently, he was arrested for exploiting under-aged tugrapian camels. It's said he has a weakness for camel toe.'

The Zeet generals stared at the man aghast.

'Zillian is a master of war,' Zeus continued. ' We must assume he will have sentinel drones in position. He will respond to an incursion with utmost force. Find his drones, and we find Zillian.'

'What do you propose we do after we find him?' Zorb asked. 'Zillian will have his weapons ready. We have to assassinate him immediately or be killed ourselves.'

The generals examined this logic and agreed. They were going to kill their king.

'All or nothing,' General Coleus offered.

The generals nodded.

'I propose we send three armed cruisers with combat teams,' Zeus said. 'We launch drones toward the surface and commence our search. Zillian must react to the presence of the drones or risk being found. He will fire on the drones, thus revealing his position.'

'Once he is located, we will beam a message requesting his surrender,' Zeus stated.

'And if he fails to comply?' Zorb asked.

'We hit him,' Zeus said. 'And hit him hard. If he survives the first volley of fire, he'll shoot back. We can't afford this turning this into a messy drawn-out fight. The action must be fast and clean.'

'You're describing a full saturation attack,' Zorb intoned. 'I suppose it's the only way to protect ourselves and prevent him escaping, just to attack us from another position.'

'Correct,' Zeus told him. 'It also means we need to employ our hardest hitting generals.'

'I will command one of the cruisers,' General Zeus announced. 'Who wants the other two?'

'I want one,' Zorb announced. Zorb may be a prick, but he was good in a fight.

'Good,' Zeus told him. 'Anyone else?'

'I'll take the other,' Coleus told them.

The generals did not like that idea. Coleus was a decent enough Zeet, but he was not a fighting man.

'No, I will do it,' Groutian Zeet said. Groutian was the king's brother-in-law and brother of the queen.

'Are you sure you want this?' Zeus asked.

'Zillian must be put down,' Groutian told him. 'And I have killed more enemies of Zeetland than all you put together.'

The generals couldn't argue with that. Groutian Zeet was one bad-ass motherfucker.

A Zeet communications officer entered the room.

'General Zeus!' Hhe announced. 'We have just received a communication from the Galactic Council. They wish to speak to King Zillian.'

'I'll bet they fucking do!' Zeus said. 'Bring them up on the screen.'

'Get the cruisers ready for combat,' Zeus told the generals. 'We must depart within the hour. I'll buy us some time with the council.'

Later that night, the Zeet fleet came out of hyperspace near the Nug solar system. They moved into position in low orbit around BeSkor and launched two dozen search drones.

BeSkor had formed over billions of years and looked very similar to prehistoric Earth. There were thousands of planets like BeSkor in the galaxy, many of which were declared natural havens and protected from abuse by casino developers and mining interests.

As such her jungles, bright blue oceans and inland lakes remained pristine.

Just as General Zeus predicted, Zillian Zeet was not going to make this mission easy for the generals.

Zillian had taken his cruiser to the bottom of a deep inland lake near the centre of a large land mass. The only indication he was there was a reed-thin communications antennae that connected him to his surveillance sentinels, positioned on the surrounding mountain tops.

The sentinels were set to scan for aircraft heat signatures, radio communication emissions or other transmitting devices. If a craft flew into their airspace, a narrow-beam flash signal was to be sent to Zillian's submerged star ship.

For two days the drones searched their assigned sectors and found nothing. On the third day, a drone flew over Zillian's lake.

Hidden under foliage on the nearby mountains, two sentinels watched it fly overhead, and beamed a signal to Zillian's cruiser.

'They're here,' Zillian Zeet announced.

His crew, by this point, knew they were fugitives. Word had spread throughout the ship they were part of an illegal action on Earth and were being hunted.

Zillian saw their guarded glances and heard some of their whispers.

He also knew his crew were loyal to him through fear alone. He was not a liked leader, and fear was not a strong enough incentive to ensure long-term loyalty. Especially considering the fact he had made these honest men part of his criminal act without their knowledge or consent.

In combat, Zillian rationalised, hiding was only ever a temporary solution. It had a dangerously eroding effect on morale. The ship could endure a long siege, but the mental state of the crew wouldn't.

Zillian guessed he didn't have long before the crew would rebel. He needed to take action.

***

'This is not working!' General Zorb told Zeus. 'We have scanned every inch of the planet and found no trace of him. How can we be sure he's even here? You know Zillian, he could have launched toward this system, then diverted elsewhere.'

Zeus couldn't argue with that logic, but something deep inside him knew Zillian was down there. Call it intuition if you will, but Zeus knew he was right.

'Two more days,' he said. 'If we can't find him here, we'll never find him.'

Zeus was due to speak to the Galactic Council again. Admiral Gustov's patience was wearing thin and the man did not hide the fact that direct galactic intervention was imminent.

'Get Gustov on the line,' Zeus told his comms officer.

A minute later, the Admiral was on-screen.

'Admiral Gustov,' Zeus began. 'I thank you for your patience. We are still searching for Zillian, but haven't found any trace at this point. We request two more days.'

'If Zillian has planted himself on the bottom of a lake or an ocean, you'll never find him. Your star cruisers can survive for months under the sea. If he sends out hunting parties for food, we're talking years.'

'I think you overestimate Zillian's capacity to stay submerged, Admiral. Give me two more days and I'll flush him out,' Zeus requested.

'Fine! You have two more days,' Admiral Gustov replied. 'Then the council will try him in absentia. You will need to return to Zeetland and sort out your nation's leadership structure, General, or the council will do it for you.'

Admiral Gustov vanished from the screen and an ad for Yetsie Cola appeared. The famous trio of Rebados monkeys started singing and dancing while riding a huge yellow banana. All three were drinking great guzzles of cola. Of course, being monkeys, they got it everywhere.

The hilarity was lost on Zeus.

Why the fuck did we sell advertising rights on the galactic council airways, he wondered in anger.

'Get all the generals on comms-link,' Zeus told his aide. 'I have a plan.'

One hour later, every drone, shuttle, supply transport and garbage barge that could fly was deployed to the surface from all three Zeet cruisers.

At an altitude of 100,000 feet, the entire drone fleet together beamed a broad and powerful radio signal to the surface.

Drone Z1287-D was tracking along its assigned waypoint across the centre of a large southern land mass, that included an inland lake, when the broadcast commenced.

"Attention, King Zillian," the message hailed. "This is your brother-in-law, General Zorb. I have a cruiser and am preparing to rescue you. The Galactic Council wants to put you on trial, but I have established an exile for you in the Orion Galaxy. I have forty greige in bullion and safe passage."

In his private cabin, Zillian read the message. Of all his generals, Zorb was the only one he trusted. But he also knew Zorb was a practical Zeet, and a patriot. *Is he working for his king? Or for the safety and security of Zeetland?*

'What do our sentinels read?' Zillian asked his Number One.

'They have only detected the message drone, sir,' he replied.

'What is the mood of the crew?' Zillian asked bluntly.

Number One hesitated.

'I thought as much,' Zillian said.

Zillian read the message again.

'It appears we have little choice. Prepare the ship for flight,' Zillian ordered.

In deep space Zeus heard the message he was hoping for.

'Sir, we have movement!' the flight officer yelled.

'Show me,' Zeus commanded.

On the holographic map, Zeus watched Zillian's ship emerge from the lake and hover just above the surface.

'General Zorb, you know if he detects us, he'll run. He'll hit his hyperdrive and disappear for good,' Zeus warned. 'The only way Zeetland can survive is to destroy that ship.'

'I concur. I know what we have to do,' Zorb said in a voice of steel.

'Weapons officer! Target Zillian's ship. Full spectrum phasers and torpedoes.' Zeus gave the order, and over the comms, he heard Zorb do the same. 'Fire at will.'

'We're being targeted!' Zillian's Number One yelled.

But before Zillian could give an order, his ship was struck with a massive bolt of high-density electromagnetic energy. The ship staggered in flight and lost most its power.

'Submerge!' Zillian yelled.

The flight crew wrestled for control of the ship, as they dumped all their remaining power to let the 50,000-ton cruiser drop like a stone back toward the surface of the lake.

'Brace!' The flight officer yelled.

In a mighty crash, the ship hit the water and began to sink, hoping for temporary safety in the depths of the lake.

This action, however, was futile as a dozen hypersonic nuclear torpedoes were racing toward them.

'Damage report!' Zillian ordered.

'Sir! The hull is secure, but we have lost—'

The man was cut off mid-sentence when the first torpedo found its target. Zillian Zeet counted four more massive hits until the command deck vaporised into flames and a confetti of metal.

With their reactor still running at war-capacity, the cooling system ruptured. Without coolant, the cruiser's nuclear reactor began rapidly over-heating. Thirty seconds later, it went critical and exploded in a massive expanding balloon of blue light.

Nobody onboard the attacking Zeet cruisers spoke as they watched the eruption of energy disintegrate the huge lake, sending vast clouds of water vapour and bedrock high into the atmosphere. They had won the engagement, but in doing so had killed their king.

The Zeet fleet watched in silence for a few more seconds before General Zeus gave the order.

'Take us home, Number One,' he said. 'Comms! Get me Admiral Gustov and standby to play him the video.'

***

Six months later, Earth had become what could only be described as very boring.

America's foreign wars had ended, and politics had become very dull under the new transparency laws. Fox

News stopped broadcasting, political lobbyists got new jobs at Home Depot, or became Uber drivers, and the military was downsized to a peace-time defence force.

Political campaigns became some guy or gal speaking into a can from an upturned apple box. They spoke about all the sensible government stuff that nobody cared about. It was the way politics was meant to be, boring and unwatchable.

Without industry-fuelled governmental corruption and waste, the US became rich. The people were paid well, taxes came down, and amazing new waterparks went up everywhere.

People kept asking, 'What's with all these fucking waterparks?' But there was no real answer.

Back on the *Blue*, Team Kenny was enjoying a special meal of spiced Whoolickian irony crustations. These wise-guy crustations were notorious for taking party jokes that one step too far, until they were finally disenfranchised and became a favourite table meal.

To mark the end of a long mission, the engineering crew made huge quantities of galactic moonshine, selling it for ching-ching and sexual favours. Kenny and James knew that while Alicia was with them, the supply of hooch would never run out.

'Cheers to you!' Kenny toasted his crew. 'The best fake political consultants in the galaxy.'

The team looked very pleased with themselves and gave a big cheer.

'In saying that, I'm sorry to break up the party. We have one more surface mission,' Kenny told them.

His team stopped drinking and stared at him. *What the fuck do we have to do now? Didn't we just save Earth?*

'The military industrial complex criminals are all still practicing evil on Earth,' Kenny told them. 'It's just a matter of time before they re-group and start their shit again.'

Alicia's mind filled with a dozen fun ways they could put the willies up them. Rebekah, Amanda and Kylie didn't really give a shit. They just wanted more Earthling booze and poontang.

'Our options are; we could abduct and brain transfer them,' Kenny offered, 'or we could pay them a personal visit.'

'I vote a personal visit,' Rebekah announced with great enthusiasm. She was as horny as a castaway pole dancer and wanted one more night on the surface.

'Personal visit,' Alicia agreed, but she still hated Rebekah.

'James, you stay on the ship as support officer,' Kenny told him.

'I really hate you, Kenny,' James told him. 'Why am I always the one left behind?'

'Because you're the only person here who knows how the phones work,' Alicia told him, trying to sound reassuring.

'I knew when you volunteered me to attend that phone course it would end badly. Gods darn it!' James swore.

'Cheer up, James. Have another crab,' Kenny offered him a fine-looking crustacean.

'Fuck your crab, Kenny. Fuck it good!' James swore again.

This made everyone laugh and James started to cry.

'Would you like to hold my dead fart rabbit, James?' Rebecca asked him, trying to be kind.

For the remainder of the day, Team Kenny set about monitoring communications between Leo Spleetz and the other key members of the MIC.

Team Kenny's intercepted communications proved the MIC men had taken a huge loss from the shift in US politics and they were hurting.

But like all wounded carnivores, they were far from defeated. Their losses had made them more determined than ever to regain their power and wealth.

As Team Kenny listened, Leo Spleetz and Sharp-and-Dangerous set about organising a covert conference with their MIC conspirators. They booked-out an entire resort on a remote island in the Philippines. Then they booked their hookers and arranged the flights.

Team Kenny viewed the resort and were highly impressed. As an added bonus, the hookers were mostly working swimwear and lingerie models. Alicia smiled using all her teeth; she sailed in whichever way the wind blew and mixing business with pleasure was not beneath her.

Kenny viewed her and shuddered. 'Okay, team, here's the plan,' he told them.

***

Sharp-and-Dangerous stood on the beach close to the resort runway. From there he watched five Lear jets land in succession and taxi toward the apron.

It took some doing to choreograph the gathering of these pedantic and miserable old men. Each had a litany of demands ranging from specific sheet fabrics, to scented slippers and flower arrangements.

Then there were the diet restrictions. This included food for men with liver disfunction, brain fog, and low libidos.

Despite them all being a major pain in his arse, Sharp-and-Dangerous formed a rare smile. He was excited their conference was about to start. Over the next few days, these men would draft a plan to restore sanity to the United States and bring back the Republican brand of power to the military.

The MIC men disembarked their jets and were greeted by, ?? who they thought, were their assigned hostesses.

The MIC men were very specific about needing some "me" time before the conference started. "Me" time for a group of malignant narcissists suffering a range of anti-social personality disorders only meant one thing: cocaine and hookers.

The night before, the Seabertian abduction teams had abducted the hookers Sharp-and-Dangerous had hired for the MIC men. They were brain transferred and dropped in a small, mostly church-going town in Alabama. Their new brain data inspired them to forget selling their pretty little arses and seek Jesus. Over the following weeks all of them became pretentious little Jesus freaks and gained a good forty pounds in weight.

On the island, Alicia, Rebekah, Amanda, Kyle and Kenny had taken their places.

Sharp-and-Dangerous knew two of the MIC men were as gay as meatballs, and had also hired two male hooker-models.

Team Kenny had little trouble changing their looks to match the abducted models, as all models looked roughly the same.

'Dumb it down, team,' Kenny told them. 'Lots of giggling, titty shaking and arse wiggling. Especially you, Kyle.'

'Fuck you, Kenny,' Kyle told him. He wasn't actually homophobic; he just didn't want to be some old fat guy's arse-boy.

The girls giggled at him, and Kyle sucked his thumb.

Team Kenny were now lined up on the runway in golf carts wearing tiny swimsuits. They watched as the first Lear jet landed and taxied into its assigned gate.

'Go, girl!' Alicia encouraged. 'Have fun!'

Amanda grinned and made her way to the foot of the boarding ladder. She greeted the old MIC as he waddled down the stairs and escorted him to the golf cart.

She chatted with the man while his luggage was onboarded to the cart, then whisked him off to his villa.

'One down, four to go!' Kenny announced. 'Next one might be yours, Kyle.'

'I hope you get arse-raped, Kenny,' Kyle snapped.

Amanda had reached the villa with her MIC. She offered him a cocktail as servants collected his luggage.

'Would you like a massage before the cocktail party?' Amanda asked her MIC.

The MIC guy was about sixty, but not the fit kind. He was short, chubby and bald. Amanda was six foot tall, young and physically perfect from head to toe.

To a non-narcissist, the physical disparity between them would have been alarming. But the MIC man didn't give a shit.

He was however a little nervous, and took a long pull on his cocktail that nearly choked him. He somewhat recovered, smiled and nodded like a small dog.

In the tropical-themed master suite, Amanda asked her MIC to take a shower.

He wasted no time under the water and returned in a robe.

Amanda was ready for him. She stood in the centre of the room holding up a glowing orb in both hands.

'Look into the orb,' Amanda told him, as it projected all the colours of the rainbow, until finally settling on brilliant aquamarine.

The man became transfixed by the orb and lost all sense of time and space.

'Watch the wall,' she told him.

The orb flashed a few times, then projected a video collage of all the horrible things the MIC had done in his career as a weapons' maker.

The images showed the faces of all the people his weapons had killed from the sale of arms. The images rolled on for several minutes; face after face, with all the blood and tears that followed. The orb continued to show the politicians he had corrupted, and the people whose lives he had destroyed. It was essentially a lifetime of pure misery and evil.

When the show was over the orb switched off, and Amanda placed it back in her bag.

Her MIC stood immobile in the centre of the room.

'You'll need to sleep now,' she told him.

He obediently made his way to the bed and lay down. His dreams were not good as he lay twitching and sweating.

Amanda left the villa and drove her cart to the Team Kenny rendezvous point. She was feeling ill from what she had seen, and a long, heavy tear ran down her face.

Alicia was assigned to escort Leo Spleetz.

She was not as humane with her MIC as Amanda. By the time Alicia was finished with Leo Spleetz, he would never function as a man again. Nor would he ever have the capacity to string a coherent sentence together.

With their mission complete, Team Kenny made their way to the beach and boarded an awaiting space uber.

'New York city, driver,' Kenny told the pilot. 'These here motherfuckers want to get wasted!'

Everyone clapped, including Alicia.

By five p.m., none of the guests had arrived at the conference cocktail party. Sharp-and-Dangerous became immediately concerned and made his way to his master's villa.

There he found Leo Spleetz curled up in a ball sucking his thumb. Within the hour he discovered all the MICs were in roughly the same condition.

Then he heard a noise outside. He ran out and discovered the servants were in a state of heightened anxiety.

'UFO!' Someone was yelling. 'We just saw a UFO!'

'It took off from the beach! I saw it on the beach!' another person was screaming.

It was then that Sharp-and-Dangerous realised the hosts and hostesses were gone.

He considered this dramatic turn of events and quickly realised he was well and truly beaten. Beaten at a game he had no real chance of winning.

'Looks like it's time for me to write my book,' he told himself and went to pack his bags.

***

Todd Splick read the latest rating report on *Reality Earth* TV channel and immediately lost his cravings for olikian coffee.

Earth had become as boring as Qui`shan batshit, and it was time to pull the plug.

'We can't grumble. It was an incredible run,' Splick told Geon.

Geon had made quintillions of ching-ching in advertising dollars yet a sad, lonely tear rolled down his cheek. The Reality Earth show was his baby, and he felt a deep sadness to lose it. 'What will we do now?' he asked Splick.

The two men had been working together on the *Reality Earth* project for some eighteen months now, and what started as a purely olikian induced dick smooching arrangement, had blossomed into a love affair.

In fact, they decided to get married, so they went on the mega-popular *First my dick, then my heart* gay relationship reality TV show.

'Check this out,' Splick announced and flashed up a brand new planet on his big TV.

Geon edged closer to his man.

'Galactic Galacom has just signed a contract for the broadcasting rights of an emerging plant near Vlock, in the Skleem system,' Spick told him. 'The beings there are huge reptilians and have just smelted iron.'

'Oh, my Gods!' Geon exclaimed. 'The smelting of iron can only lead to one thing.'

'I know, right?' Splick continued. 'Now wait for it; they have also formed a weird new religion. Not as stupid as Christianity mind you, but it's still pretty weird. They call it the holy trinity, with a horny dog, a foul-tempered dragon, and a really stupid talking goat with a lisp.

Anyway, shit's about to get real for the next thousand years.'

'Brilliant!' Geon told him. 'What will we name it?'

'Hmm, how aboutPlanet Todd?' He suggested.

'Love it! Planet Todd it is!' Geon knew the name sucked, yet he faked enthusiasm for his lover. 'I'll start calling some sponsors. Maybe some pet-care companies will sponsor the horny dog, and home insurers for that shitty dragon. Farmers love fucking goats, so Big Ag will want in.'

Geon Plume knew he was on a winner, and there was a dune-buggy adventure moon with a great casino close to his house he wanted to buy.

Three years later

Planet Khentimentiu
in the Rheel system
City of Clusso-Lude,
the United Galactic Seat of Government
Monday Morning — about nine a.m.

To say Clusso-Lude was a government town was like saying a 2029 Bentley was nicer to drive than a 1979 Datsun 180B.

And as a government town, for five days each week, life in Clusso-Lude was as boring as Messturian batshit. Mondays especially took a deep dive into serious misery.

This was because the resident galactic ambassadors, planetary representatives, solicitors, clerks and other lesser officials spent their weekends drinking red wine and eating cheese.

Come Monday, they were all hungover, constipated, and more than a little foul tempered.

'What's on the roster?' Chamber Parliamentary Whip Fross asked his small and overly enthusiastic clerk, a man named Mleek.

'Yes, sir! Today, we have the application for planet Earth to become recognised as dignified,' Mleek told his boss.

'Earth? You mean that lunatic asylum on TV?' Fross asked.

'Ex-lunatic asylum, sir. They have recently become as boring as Langerhaul whale piss after tossing their Republican politics,' Mleek corrected his boss.

Whip Fross had lost all interest in Earth after they shut down the *Reality Earth* show.

'Then tell me, Mr Mleek, how in the name of my once proud flaccid penis did this bullshit get on my ticket?'

Fross was a famous red wine drinker and a renowned cheese eater. So much so, his Monday hangovers had ruined the careers of many a good intern and clerk.

'Apparently, a couple of years ago, the Seabertians conducted a unilateral campaign to help them.' Mleek was also a keen cheese eater and had consumed too much of the new fungus-enriched blurk varietal.

Mleek let go a small fart that was very nearly followed by a shart.

'Sorry, sir,' Mleet said.

'Unilateral? Is that even legal?' Fross asked, getting ready to slap his clerk.

'Kind of, sir. But it was Earth, so nobody really gave a toss,' Mleek replied.

'Fucking Seabertians! They think they're the Gods' gift just because they're tall and pretty,' Fross declared. 'Motherfuckers. So, what happened?'

'Ah, yes,' Mleek checked his notes. 'The Seabertians removed a major political element on Earth called Republicans. This movement was designed and built to keep everyone extremely stupid. It appears that without this political influence the Earthlings got their collective shit together and are now dignified. Just like us.'

Mleek farted again.

'Ha! Dignified like us! That'll be the fucking day!' Fross scoffed.

'The Earth delegation advocates are waiting in the foyer. Shall I bring them in?' Mleek asked.

'I've got to tell you, Mleek. You are one smelly little fungus-cheese eater,' Fross continued. 'Bringing me an Earth delegation on a Monday would normally get you flogged.'

'Yes, sir, Mondays really suck,' Mleek agreed.

Fross sighed and shook his head.

'Fuck it! Bring them in,' Fross intoned with pure loathing.

Fighting new legislation through the political quagmire that is the Galactic governmental swamp is a time consuming and soul crushing experience.

Finally, after five more Earth years, and millions of galactic greekos spent, the Galactic Council voted in a highly regulated and monitored version of an Earth Assimilation Programme.

No one in the galactic chambers cheered. Many thought it was 50/50 the whole thing would go tits-up in the first six months, and the pro-Earth delegation was simply too exhausted to be happy.

Sometimes in life, the fight is so dirty, victory becomes meaningless.

Planet Earth

Alicia woke from her sleepover in Kenny's New York apartment.

She still thought of Kenny as her sex toy, and a convenient bit of fun when there was nothing better to do. Though, she was developing what could be described as an embryo of something that may include the very early stages of an emotional attachment for him.

What she really loved was his apartment with its views of Central Park and a parking garage. There was also a great gym and keto/paleo eatery downstairs. Alicia liked to work her thighs and butt for an hour or so, then grab a low-carb brunch.

She would then call Hann, her Swedish body builder masseuse, to give her a massage. She had trained Hann to go deep-tissue, then finish her off with a nice little pea tickle.

Alicia shivered at the memory.

She jumped out of bed and bounced toward the bathroom. Alicia liked to bounce and she tended to bounce wherever she went.

Mid-bounce, Kenny's phone rang and she grabbed it.

'What?' She said into the phone.

'Is that how Star Corp taught you to answer a Gods darn telephone?' Admiral Gustov asked her.

'Oh, oh fuck!' She stammered. 'Sorry, Admiral. I'll get Commander Kendrick.'

'Put some clothes on, you skinny skank!' The Admiral ordered before Alicia realised it was a video call.

'Eeek!' She said and threw the phone at Kenny who was still fast asleep.

'Hey! What the—'

'Shut up, Kendrick!' The Admiral told him. 'Your little holiday is over. They granted Earth dignified status and you have work to do.'

Kenny sat up and stared at the phone.

'Dignified!' He said to himself, as he watched Alicia's arse twerk while she brushed her teeth. 'Fucking woman dances even when she's brushing her teeth!'

'What?' Admiral Gustov asked.

'Nothing, sir.'

One week later...

Sergeant Lisa placed the transport in stealth mode, hovering at 1500 feet above the White House West Wing car park.

'That's her,' Lieutenant Rick announced as they watched a tall, red-haired woman exit the West Wing and enter the back seat of a black town car.

The woman was tall and fit, Lieutenant Rick saw. *She's likely going to be trouble*, he told himself.

The aliens followed the car as it merged into traffic and edged its way along K Street heading toward Georgetown.

It was 11 p.m. and the traffic was light, so the trip was pretty fast. Once there, the tall lady exited the car and went inside.

'Okay, guys,' Rick said. 'Her name is Rachel Green and she's the president's chief of staff. We need to grab her and get her back to the ship with as little fuss as possible.'

'What if she puts up a fight? Can we hit her?' Alicia asked.

'No. No hitting,' Rick told her.

'What about a taser? Can we taser her?' Alicia enquired further.

'Tasers leave burns. No tasering. Stun-guns only.'

Alicia hated stun-guns. They were way too fast and efficient for her liking; one quick zap and the Earthlings went down.

Experience had taught Rick that going on operations with Alicia required great patience. He also knew she was Commander Kendrick's little favourite, thus was forced to endure her.

In turn, Alicia hated Rick. She had already devised a cunning plan to lure him into an airlock using her sweet, sweet boobies, then blow him out into space. All she needed was the right moment.

'Let's get Ms. Green back to the ship unharmed,' Rick affirmed.

Alicia grunted.

The aliens waited another hour until they saw Green's bedroom light go out. Sergeant Lisa flew the transport down to the middle of quiet road and placed it in a hover.

The hatch of the ship opened and the abduction team jumped out onto the road. The secret service agent stationed in front of the house saw this and froze in shock.

As he attempted to yell something until Alicia fired her phaser and he collapsed.

'Good shot,' Rick told her.

'Whatever,' she muttered, still hating him.

The aliens phasered a second secret service man on the stairs, jimmied the locks, and went inside. They quietly made their way into the house using the Jimmy Wong All-Galactic-Door-Opener they had bought online for just $9.99.

The team silently moved through the house until they found Rachel Green's bedroom. Rick glanced into her room and quickly pulled his head back.

'Bugger,' Rick breathed.

Rachel Green was still wide awake and reading her Kindle. Rick was well aware that she had a military background and was raised with four older brothers. This resume` made her particularly dangerous.

He also knew they couldn't delay, as two secret service were laid out in the street below.

He took a deep breath and stepped into the room.

Rachel Green looked up and saw the aliens. Without hesitation, she threw the kindle hard and fast. It raced through the air and hit Alicia between the eyes. Alicia grunted once and went down.

Rick, slightly shocked by this, fired his phaser late as Green rolled off the bed, scooping up the Sig. 9mm she kept under the pillow.

Green fired two well-aimed shots. One round nicked Rick's right ear, and the second hit him square in the chest.

Rick made an oomph-like sound and flew backward. landing on the floor. Green jumped to her feet and raced toward her attackers.

The abduction team's standard issue uniform was made from Ralopian neo-glist fiber, and the bullet that hit Rick had deflected harmlessly away. As Green came into view, he fired his phaser and she dropped like a stone.

Alicia regained consciousness and sat up, viewing the scene.

'Told you we should have tasered her,' she said, as blood trickled down her face.

Rick stared at her for a second. 'What a goat-rope,' he muttered.

It was no mean feat for the injured aliens to get Rachel Green down the stairs and into the transport as the woman was one hundred and fifty pounds of muscle.

'What the fuck was that?' Lisa asked. 'Did I hear gunshots?'

'Just drive the fucking bus, Lisa,' Alicia told her.

Onboard the *Mercurial Blue*, they placed Rachel Green in what the Seabertians called the wake-up room.

Years of experience proved that if abductees woke up on a table surrounded by aliens, they tended to freak out, scream like banshees, then pass-out.

It took drugs and an hour of comforting to calm them down.

To avoid all that nonsense, they had built a special room that looked like a library. A nice calming library with lots of books and a desk with a green lamp shade. Earthlings loved green-shaded library lamps for some reason.

Soothing classical music was also piped into the room.

Rachel Green was placed on a chair with her head resting on a desk. There she suddenly woke up and looked around.

She assumed she was still dreaming, but it all seemed so real. As she watched, an older man approach in a well-tailored business suit. He was tall and trim, with a friendly face and a close-trimmed grey beard.

Rachel Green immediately knew the man. It was Morgan Freeman.

'Do you mind if I take a seat, young lady?' Morgan Freeman asked, really getting into character.

Green sat stupefied by this very weird dream. Yet, it was very compelling.

'Do you know where you are?' Morgan Freeman asked her.

Rachel looked around and shook her head. She decided there was no chance in hell she was going to actively participate in some stupid dream. *If my brain wants to put on some half-arsed pantomime, fine. But I am not going to help it.*

'Now, Rachael, I am about to do something a little bit surprising,' Morgan Freeman told her. 'Please don't be afraid.'

Mr Freeman always has the best manners, Green acknowledged. *His voice is so soothing and reassuring.*

As she watched, Morgan Freeman picked a TV remote controller and pressed a button. One whole wall of the library morphed from a wall of books into a view of the Earth from deep space.

Rachel stared at the view, then at Morgan, and back to the view again. A doubt formed in her head that this was not actually a dream, so she pinched herself. Ouch!

Not good, a voice in her head reported back.

She then saw this was not a static view. The Earth was slowly turning in the window.

'What the...' she moaned.

'Okay, then,' Morgan Freeman told her. 'Here we go, are you ready?'

Rachel shook her head.

'I am about to confirm everything you think you know about aliens and UFOs,' Morgan Freeman announced and smiled at her. 'Would you like some tea?'

Rachel stared blankly at the man. The scale of what was happening was began to sink in.

'Can I take off this mask now?' Morgan Freeman asked her. 'We thought it would make you feel more comfortable, but it's really hot under here.'

Green failed to answer as the man took off his mask. After all the shit she had already seen tonight, this didn't really surprise her. After all, she was floating in space onboard an alien star ship. What could possibly surprise her now?

The tea arrived.

'Black, no sugar,' Admiral Gustov, the now ex-Morgan Freeman, told her. 'Let's start at the beginning. But first, I'd like to introduce my associate.'

A door whirred open and Kenny entered the room.

'May I introduce Commander Kendrick,' the admiral told her.

Rachel knew his face. He was the man who ran the Earl for President campaign that blew-up the Republican Party. What the fuck was he doing here? She asked herself.

Kenny smiled at Rachel, who offered him a twisted grimace in return.

'Rachel, you are about to play a major role in what your people call First-Contact.' Admiral Gustov told her. 'We request a secret meeting with your president, and the process will begin.'

Rachel Green sipped her tea. It was the best peppermint tea she had ever tasted, and was not remotely surprised the aliens knew it was her favourite.

She then took a moment to say a silent prayer of thanks the Democrats had won the election. She shuddered at the thought of an advanced alien race meeting the recent crop of GOP presidents.

'Can I use the bathroom, please?' She asked.

'Sure. It's the first door on the left,' Kenny told her. 'Mind the soap dispenser, it's a bit splashy.'

One month later
The School of Anthropology, University of Arizona

Dr Jennifer-Louise Laker was closing her post graduate lecture on behavioural evolution which focused on how the United States Republican Party were able to erode the requirement for governmental truth and integrity as essential elements in their political modus operandi.

'Your assigned paper will describe in detail the de-evolution of American intelligence in relationship to the post-modern current political environment. I want a focus on how forty percent of God-fearing Americans remained devoted to the Republican Party, a political movement that eliminated all of the most fundamental elements of ethics and principles,' she told her class.

As her students left the lecture room, Dr Laker noticed a man she hadn't seen before seated at the back.

'May I help you?' She asked.

'As a matter of fact, Doctor Laker,' the man began, 'You are in a position to help all of us.'

Thirty minutes later, Dr Laker was strapped into the back seat of a Blackhawk helicopter heading for Area 51, deep in the Nevada desert. She told the man that she didn't have a travel bag.

'Where you're going, we'll give you a special one,' the man told her.

As the chopper approached the base, Dr Laker saw a lot of activity on the ground. Choppers were landing and taking off from a dozen landing pads. 737 passenger jets were unloading people and equipment, and armed soldiers in white helmets were everywhere.

Dr Laker's Blackhawk landed, and she was escorted to an awaiting jeep. Without fuss or ceremony, the jeep whisked her along the airport apron and into a large open hangar.

There she saw over one hundred people seated in three rows, including many faces she knew from the academic world. She suddenly realised how hot and dusty the air was, as her escort offered her a water bottle, then got her seated.

All the civilians present looked somewhat confused, but not a little excited. They all knew whatever was coming had to be big.

Sirens could be heard approaching the hangar and the presidential motorcade swung into sight. Seconds later, the secret service escorted the president of the United States into the hangar, along with a bevy of other men in dark suits.

The president wasted no time in walking up to the lectern and commenced his address.

'Welcome everyone,' he began. 'It looks like we've got your attention.'

There were a few nervous chuckles.

'I bet you all want to know why we've gone to the extraordinary effort to gather the nation's top astrophysicists, anthropologists, psychologists, biologists, linguistics, and engineers?' The president asked. 'The answer is simple. We have made first contact with our neighbours in the galaxy.'

The shock hit home, and everyone in the room stopped breathing.

Regardless of what they may have said publicly, every scientist there had spent many a long hour considering the ramifications of first contact.

They all knew that numerically, based on the trillions of stars in the galaxy, extra-terrestrial life must exist. Many also knew it was just a matter of time before we were formally introduced.

The technical, medical, economic, and social changes that must occur post first contact would take mankind to levels thought impossible.

'Can you imagine an advanced alien civilisation tolerating capitalism?' Many had asked. 'A system that provides sociopaths the legal protection to steal the national wealth.'

"For a species and its host planet to survive more than two centuries post-industrialisation," Joshua Kimmel wrote, "advanced races eventually morphed into an egalitarian culture. One where individual greed is eliminated and replaced by mutually beneficial productivity. All while being in complete harmony with their natural world."

Essentially the polar opposite of how industrialised human-kind exists on Earth.

'You are all selectees for the Presidential Panel on First Contact,' the president continued. 'It is you who will be game planning how we do this. You will be meeting with the alien representatives to build a roadmap for our future. Any questions?'

In the wide space between the president's podium and the seated scientists, a Seabertian transport de-activated stealth mode.

The assembled men and women stood and viewed the glowing oblong as it hovered a foot off the floor. Some in the group surged backward and a few chairs were knocked over. But most stood still and gazed at the wonder in front of them.

The spacecraft hatch opened and six Seabertians stepped out.

'Okay then,' Kenny announced and gave the Earthlings a little wave. 'Here we go.'

'This is really going to suck,' Alicia told him.

Rebecca saw that Kyle was getting nervous, so she held him close.

'Suck your thumb, Kyle,' she told him.

The End